Catch the Passing Breeze

Holt, Rinehart and Winston · *New York*

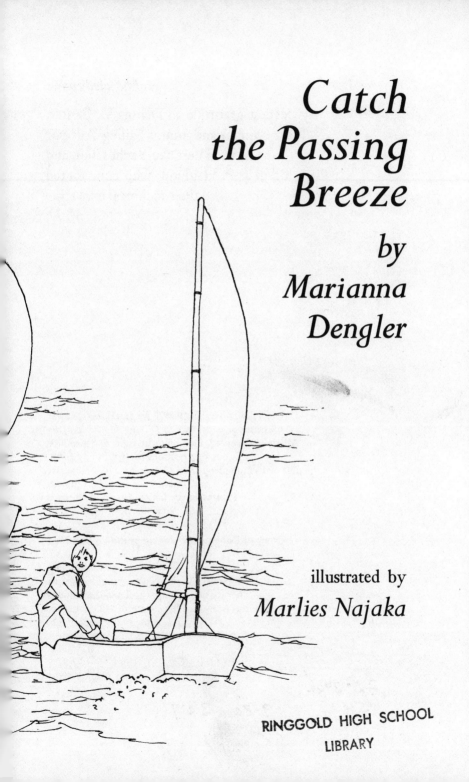

Catch the Passing Breeze

by

Marianna Dengler

illustrated by

Marlies Najaka

Acknowledgment

My deepest gratitude to Dennis V. Parker,
Fleet Captain and Junior Sailing Advisor
of the Westlake Yacht Club, and
Bradley P. Haglund, who contributed
their technical expertise.

M. D.

Text copyright © 1977 by Marianna Dengler
Illustrations copyright © 1977 by Marlies Najaka
All rights reserved, including the right to reproduce
this book or portions thereof in any form.
Published simultaneously in Canada by Holt, Rinehart
and Winston of Canada, Limited.
Printed in the United States of America
10 9 8 7 6 5 4 3 2 1

Library of Congress Cataloging in Publication Data
Dengler, Marianna.
Catch the passing breeze.
SUMMARY: Vicki Banyon struggles against
her mother's disapproval and the family's
poverty toward her dream of sailing a sabot
at the junior yacht club.
[1. Sailing—Fiction] I. Najaka, Marlies.
II. Title.
PZ7.D4145Cat   [Fic]   77-3159
ISBN 0-03-019426-1

To my father, with love.
M. D.

one

    Vicki stood at the end of the pier, hanging over the rail, her gaze fixed on the entrance to the big marina. No small sails were in sight, only the *White Star*, a familiar sloop coming out on its afternoon run. There were other sails on the horizon, but they were large and far away.

"You aimin' to be shark bait?" asked Zeek coming up next to her.

"Not today," she answered him absently. This aging black man in the red knit cap was as familiar here as the sea gulls, but more than that, he was Vicki's friend.

Vicki clung to the rail, her blond hair flying, her slender body leaning far out over the water.

"You get down before you fall in!" Zeek warned.

She looked back at his wrinkled black face and grinned. Her secret dreams were safe with him, and so was she. He was her protector here on the pier.

Over Zeek's shoulder, Vicki could see the famous Venice, California beach, and beyond that, the faded and peeling apartments which lined the coast. On the right of the entrance to the pier stood the battered bait shop, and on the left was Sally's, a run-down bar and grill.

In summer, the beach teemed with people and helicopters kept close watch from the sky. Now only the fishermen remained, scattered along the length of the pier, waiting gladly for the whim of the fish in the surf below.

"Vicki!" called Zeek. "Get down!"

"If I fall in," she said, "you can just reel me back up."

She eyed the pole in his hand and the empty fish bucket between them. "You're not catchin' much else today."

Zeek was the boat crane operator, but when there were no boats to raise or lower, he fished.

"There's a fine perch waitin' down there," he said.

She turned back to the sea. It sparkled in the clear October sunlight. The sight of it made her want to sing.

Vicki Banyon lived for the afternoons when she was free to come to the pier. She loved it all: the noisy surf, the warm sun, the fresh wind, the diving gulls that always seemed to know when the fish were biting, and even the awesome smell of old fish.

But it was the sails that made her come.

Some days, instead of coming to the pier, she crossed Washington Street on her bike and rode into another world, Marina Del Rey, down broad streets lined with yellow flowers, past expensive homes and restaurants and shops, and finally to the marina itself.

Vicki would leave her bike in the marina parking lot and wander along the docks looking at the boats—yachts really—row upon row of them, their bare masts reaching skyward, their hulls rocking gently in the water.

Whole afternoons vanished this way. If a boat came in or out of a slip nearby, she'd rush to watch, fascinated by the smoothness with which the crew handled the difficult maneuver.

Once a family of three invited her to come aboard and look around. She did, eagerly admiring the fine wood on the deck, the intricate rigging, the beauty and compactness of the cabin below . . . and then it was time for them to leave.

That night she had gone to the library and checked out every book she could find on sailing. Someday she'd know what it was like to sail.

"Here comes the *White Star*," she said to Zeek.

"Yeah," he said, "but them little boats ain't comin'."

"I know," said Vicki with disappointment.

Three weeks ago she'd been standing here with Zeek, and she'd seen them for the first time, the little boats, looking like tiny oblong tea cups propelled by tooth pick masts and match cover sails, playing near the entrance to the marina. What were they? Who sailed them? She had to find out.

On the spot, she had decided to follow them back to the marina by land and try to find their dock. She had ridden fast and found them moored next to the boathouse, all twelve sails with red wooden shoe emblems flapping in the wind.

Inside the boathouse, the instructor had been talking about sailing to the skippers, boys her age or younger.

Vicki had listened until they were done. Then she had spoken with the instructor. The boats were sabots, eight foot sailboats, and this was a junior yacht club. Best of all, the fee was only seven dollars a year!

Here was her chance! The boats were small. Maybe someday she could even own one. The skippers were young, all kids. And the money? She had four dollars saved already. She had found a way!

Now Vicki had the seven dollars. She ran her hand inside her jeans pocket and felt the folded bills. She had been back to the marina several times in the last week, only no one had been there. The next time they were in the bay, she would follow them back and join.

The *White Star* was almost in line with the pier now and coming fast, its two big sails pulled in close and full of wind. She waved, as she always did. The crew, a young man and woman, waved back. She thought the skipper looked familiar, but he was too far away to tell for sure.

Then the *White Star* changed course and came toward the pier.

"What's he up to?" said Zeek in surprise.

Vicki didn't answer. She was watching the couple work the sails. She'd read everything she could find about sailing, and now she was seeing it happen.

But why were they coming so close?

The skipper, a man with a honey colored beard and wearing a blue jacket, brought the boat within hailing distance. When he turned around to wave, she recognized him. He was the man who held the sabot classes!

The woman handling the smaller sail cupped her hands and shouted toward the pier.

"Ahoy! Girl in yellow!"

Vicki glanced down at the yellow sweater she was wearing. Then she cupped her own hands and shouted into the wind.

"Ahoy! *White Star!*"

"Want to sail?"

"Yes!" she screamed, her voice breaking from the force.

The skipper waved and began to bring the boat toward the small fishing dock under the pier.

Vicki ran to the boat crane yelling at Zeek. "Lower me down! Lower me down! Hurry!"

"Hey. Easy!" he said laughing.

"Please! Hurry!" she begged.

"You know I'm not supposed to . . ."

"Come on!"

He shrugged and began to make a sling. Quickly, Vicki climbed into it.

"Wait," said Zeek. "What about your mother?" He was holding the sling, refusing to lower it.

He was right. They both knew that for some reason her mother hated the sea and had even forbidden her to come to the pier.

"But . . . I may never get another chance!"

"Get some sense, child. From what you've told me about her, she's gonna be mad . . . *awful* mad!"

She hesitated.

"Zeek," she said. "Does she have to know?"

He studied her face.

She continued. "I'll be back before she gets home!"

He nodded.

She grabbed his hand and squeezed it against her cheek.

"Lower away," she called.

"Hang on!" he said.

Slowly he began to lower the sling.

Vicki looked down. Below her was the small fishing dock, and beside it stood the *White Star*, her sails crackling in the wind.

two

∾ Zeek landed Vicki squarely into the skipper's waiting arms. Laughing, he put her on the dock.

"Quite a drop!" he said.

"Not bad," she answered smiling. "I could have jumped!"

"Thought I recognized you," he continued. "I'm Bob Schaffer, and that's my wife, Sandy." He nodded toward the pretty young woman smiling up from the boat.

"I'm Vicki . . . Vicki Banyon," she replied.

"Ready?" He stepped into the boat and offered her his hand.

She knew the proper words.

"Request permission to come aboard, Sir," she said formally.

Bob's eyes widened with pleasure.

"Permission granted!" he said. "Come on. Let's go!"

Taking his hand and ducking the wildly swinging boom, she stepped aboard the *White Star*.

Sandy released the mooring line. Vicki saw the sails fill and felt the boat surge forward.

She waved at Zeek who stood grinning on the pier

above her, and then she looked aloft. The two white sails billowed full. The red lightning emblem and the numbers one-four-one, which she had seen so often from the pier, were now directly over her head.

"Ever sail before?" asked Bob, his hand steady on the tiller.

She shook her head.

They sailed parallel with the shoreline, the boat heeling gently toward the shore. Unfamiliar as it was, Vicki's fingers itched to hold the tiller.

They were moving fast now, the wind fierce in her face, the waves licking the low side of the boat. She felt the salt spray on her cheek.

"Fun?" said Sandy, her long dark hair glistening in the sun. Vicki realized that her face ached from grinning so long.

Then she began to ask questions, the words tumbling out of her mouth so fast she stammered. All the things she'd read about were all around her now, and she wanted to know everything—all at once!

How to come about? How to trim a sail? Port? Starboard? Tacking? All the things she'd known only as little diagrams in books were suddenly real!

"Stop!" said Bob laughing. "You can't swallow it all in one day!"

She laughed. That's exactly what she was trying to do.

"Come on back here a minute," he said.

"Me?" she asked, hoping.

"Yeah, you. Let's see if you can earn your keep."

Carefully she moved to the seat beside him.

He uncleated the mainsheet, the line that held the mainsail, and let her hold it. It was heavy from the pressure of the wind on the big sail. He had her hold the tiller. She shivered with excitement.

Then, he got up and moved to the front of the boat, leaving Vicki alone at the helm!

The big sail began to shake. Instinctively, she pulled it in.

"Good girl!" yelled Sandy. "She's a natural!"

"That's right!" yelled Bob. "Trim those sails! Catch all the passing breeze!"

Catch the passing breeze! The words sang in Vicki's mind.

Then Bob came back and took the helm, and Vicki moved to her seat in the center of the boat. They sailed on, moving now toward the horizon. Why . . . why did her mother hate the sea? There was so much about it to love. It was the one dark thing between them.

"Bob says you're joining the sabot class," said Sandy. Her voice drew Vicki back.

She nodded and patted her pocket. "I have my money right here." Then she turned to Bob. " I went back three times, but nobody was there."

"Wednesdays," he said. "We meet at the boathouse at three o'clock."

"Sabots are fun to sail," said Sandy. "Which kind do you have?"

The question was innocent, but all Vicki could do was stare. She saw Bob and Sandy exchange glances.

"Vicki," said Bob. "You didn't understand. Those

15

boats you've seen all *belong* to the kids who sail them. You gotta have a boat to join the class."

Vicki studied the sail above her head. Her arms felt limp. When she looked back at Bob he was serious.

"I tried to tell you the other day, but you ran off before I had a chance."

"But . . . but . . ." Her throat was tight. "Couldn't I just . . ."

"Tell you what. There are four more classes this fall. Sit in. See if you like it."

"But I could never . . ."

"No use investing in a boat if you don't like sailing."

Not like it? If he only knew! But how would she ever get a boat!

When they turned back toward the marina, the wind was behind them. Vicki hadn't realized that they had come such a long way out. By the position of the sun, she calculated that it must be five thirty, two hours since they had left the pier. She couldn't even see the fishing pier, but all of Los Angeles lay before her, from Point Dume, near the Malibu Beach, to the Palos Verdes Peninsula.

Bob let the mainsail all the way out so that the boom was at right angles with the boat; Sandy secured the jib sail to the other side with a long whisker pole.

"Wing and wing," said Sandy. "We're running before the wind!"

Bob motioned to Vicki to come back to the helm again.

"Sail us home!" he commanded. "I'm tired."

She had been watching him all afternoon; now, she was able to take over without a word. Bob and Sandy sat in the front of the boat talking quietly. Vicki was alone with the lowering sun and the sails, tinted pink from its glow. It was everything she had known it would be, and more.

They passed the fishing pier, empty now of fishermen. Ahead lay the breakwater, the large island at the entrance to the marina.

The sun was only a half round crimson ball when she felt a hand on her shoulder.

"I'll take it from here," Bob said gently.

Wordlessly, she handed him the tiller and moved back to her position amidships.

Sandy smiled. "The first time is always very special," she said.

Bob and Sandy brought the *White Star* into the marina, down the channels with their forests of tinkling masts, and into the slip. When they were secured at the dock, it was almost dark.

No need to hurry now. Her mother was already home. Whatever would happen was already on its way.

As they left the dock, she turned back for one last look at the *White Star*. No matter what happened tonight or tomorrow, the last few hours were hers to keep.

She helped them carry the gear to their car. Then she set down the sail bag and cushions she'd been carrying and, on an impulse, hugged Sandy and Bob each in turn.

"We'll go again," said Sandy, her eyes glistening.

"See you Wednesday, sailor," said Bob firmly.

They dropped her off at the pier to pick up her bike. By the time she reached home, it was past eight o'clock. She saw the light under the door, took a deep breath, and turned the knob.

three

 "But I had to go!" Vicki was seated at the kitchen table. Sarah Banyon stood facing her, her back to the kitchen sink.

"No," she said coldly. "You didn't."

"I didn't do it to hurt you!"

"But you did it!" Her mother's eyes snapped.

Vicki was near to tears. "Didn't you ever want something . . . so much . . . so much you thought you'd break in half if you didn't get it?"

A flash of pain crossed her mother's face. "Vicki," she said, "sailing is for the rich. In case you haven't noticed, we're not."

She motioned around the shabby, one-room apartment. "We can't even afford a telephone!"

"But today was free! I was invited!"

"Yes! And it's only made you want it more!"

That was true, but Vicki squared her shoulders.

"I just don't get it!" she said. "Why is it so wrong?"

"You disobeyed!"

"Okay. But it's not like I'm in any real trouble! Some of the kids I know . . ."

"I've explained. We can't afford it!"

"Would you rather I . . ."

"Of course not!" Her mother's face was full of anger now. "But maybe I'd know how to handle that." She paused and her voice softened. "Vicki, this is something you can *never* have."

She crossed the short space between them and sat down beside Vicki. "Little girl, when you dream too big, your dreams get all smashed."

"But Mother, if you could have been there, if you could have seen it!" She felt her mother stroking her hair.

"I know," said Sarah. "But at the other end of all those big, beautiful dreams is disappointment, heartbreak even." She paused. "I know. Believe me, I know!"

Encouraged by her mother's tenderness, Vicki asked softly, "Mother, why don't you like the sea?"

Her mother's body stiffened, and she moved away. "I've told you! Now forget it! Tomorrow you get a job. Mrs. Baker is looking for a sitter. And don't go near the pier—ever again!"

"But . . ."

"Vicki, it's over. Finished! Is that clear?"

It was.

Mother and daughter spent the rest of the evening in silence. Sarah angrily clattered the pots and pans as she finished the dishes. Then she went into the bathroom.

Vicki knew it would be an hour before her mother came out. She always hurt from the long day at work. The factory was a two mile walk each way, and the long hours bent over the assembly line conveyor belt made her back ache. Soaking in a hot bath eased her tired muscles.

Sarah Banyon was not old, but she seemed old, and she didn't smile often.

Vicki finished her science chapter, at least she turned the rest of the pages. Then she slipped out of her jeans, pulled the sweater over her head, and held it in her hands. Ahoy! Girl in yellow! She hugged the sweater and got into bed.

Vicki lay staring at the ceiling and seeing not the ceiling but her mother's eyes as they had been this evening—as they were every time there was a mention of the sea. Anger was there, certainly, but there was also something else. Fear? Pain? Vicki didn't know, and it was something Sarah couldn't or wouldn't discuss.

There was one other thing Sarah couldn't discuss— Vicki's father. Years ago, when her questions about him had become no longer avoidable, Sarah had delivered one tense lecture which had sounded to Vicki's young ears like a passage from a book. From it she had learned that he was "someone she could be proud of", that her mother had loved him very much; and that he had never seen Vicki because he had been "away" from the time she was born until his death in an auto accident when she was four.

There was so much more Vicki had wanted to know —so much, but each time she started to ask, the look on her mother's face made her stop short.

At those times, Vicki saw her mother—her rock of

security, her shield against the world's ills—struggle with some deep nameless emotion, and over the years she put away her own need to know.

She never asked about him anymore, but she couldn't erase the questions from her mind.

A long time ago, she remembered a photograph of him on her mother's chest-of-drawers. Then it wasn't there anymore. What had happened to that picture? She'd love to see it again!

Vicki heard the bathroom door and closed her eyes, pretending to be asleep. She heard footsteps moving about the room for a while, and then she felt her mother's cheek, warm on her own. She wanted to hold out her arms, as she always did, but tonight she couldn't.

When she opened her eyes again, the room was in darkness.

If only Tak were here. He would understand. He was only a year older than she, but he seemed so wise, so sure of himself. When she was with him, she felt wise and strong.

Takashi Ito was her friend, and at times, a real puzzle. He was born in Tokyo and brought here by his parents when he was four. He'd grown up here, gone to school here, roamed the streets of Venice, California, knew how to get along. But he had a gentleness, a courtesy about him that made him different.

Vicki had met Tak for the first time one afternoon on the pier about a year ago. They had lost no time discovering their mutual interest—the sea. The accidental meetings continued with greater frequency, until finally they could no longer be called accidental.

Then one morning in mid-September, Vicki had left the apartment early, sketch pad in hand, and stopped at the pier on the way to school. Next to the sea, her favorite interest was drawing; to combine the two was pure pleasure.

She had been standing there, trying to capture the flight of a gull and shivering a little, when she had felt a warm jacket tossed gently about her shoulders. It was Tak.

He had smiled his approval of her artistic effort, and they had stood there together as she finished the sketch, watching the sea change colors as the sun rose behind them. Then, without a word, they had turned back down the long pier, picked up their bikes, and continued on to school.

She needed him now! He was the only one who really knew—who shared her passion for the sails. The difference between their feelings was that Tak had a plan. He studied so that he could be a naval officer and go to sea. His whole life would be bound to the sea. Vicki had no such plan. She wasn't even a good student. Her counselor had suggested that she take cooking or some other course that didn't need much brain work.

But this day had been real. The *White Star* was real. Lying here in bed, she could feel the rocking boat, taste the salty spray on her lips, hear the sails crackle in the wind.

She listened to her mother's regular breathing from across the room. If only this dark thing weren't between them . . . if only. . . . She slept.

The alarm rang. Mother and daughter dressed silently

*They had stood there together as she
finished the sketch watching the sea change.*

in the chill air. Just as Vicki was ready to leave, her mother spoke.

"Go straight to Mrs. Baker's after school. She's expecting you."

"I will," she said tightly and went out the door, shutting it quietly behind her.

As she approached the campus, she recognized Tak's angular form and shining black hair. He was standing near the bike racks. He saw her coming and waited. Hurriedly, she locked her bike in the rack and they started off toward the classrooms.

"Where were you yesterday?" she asked, eager to tell her own news.

"Kid sister was sick again. Didn't make it to work either!"

Tak tended one of the big yachts at the marina. His job was to keep it clean, provisioned, and ready to sail so that its owner could just step aboard and go. Sometimes Tak even got to go along on the weekend outings as deck hand. Lucky Tak!

"Guess what happened at the pier!" said Vicki.

"A sea gull finally got you?" he asked grinning.

"Yuck, no!"

"Zeek caught a whale?"

She shook her head. "The *White Star*! You know."

He nodded.

"I sailed it!"

"You what?"

She told it all, and as she talked she felt his excitement growing and mixing with her own.

The warning bell rang, and they parted at the drinking fountain—each to his separate classes.

Somehow she managed to get through the day, but her mind was not on her studies. Her joy over the sail in the *White Star* and her unhappiness over the fight with her mother mingled in her brain like two frantic bees imprisoned in a jar.

Tak met her at the bike racks after school.

"To the pier, lady?"

She shook her head. "To Mrs. Baker's."

"Then your mother . . ."

Vicki thought she had herself in hand, but at the mention of her problem, tears began again.

"Thought so," said Tak. "Now what?"

"I don't know. Work mostly. After school. Saturdays." She smiled up at him. "But yesterday was real. I sailed!"

She stopped. They were in front of the Baker apartment building. "And someday . . . somehow, I'll do it again."

He took her hand, something he had never done before. Then, wordlessly, he was gone.

Vicki watched him go and felt a stirring in her heart. Then she turned and started up the apartment house steps.

four

❧ "You make the fudge!" commanded five year old Sammy. "I'll make the punch!"

Vicki and the three children were in the small kitchen of the Baker apartment.

"Come on, Vicki!" shouted Billy, the sturdy seven year old. "I'll make the popcorn."

Little Jill, four, was already into the cupboard digging out the party plates.

Vicki looked down at the three excited faces. Today was Wednesday. The sabot class was meeting. The last place she wanted to be was here with her three noisy charges. The last thing she felt like having was a party.

"Not today!" she snapped, more anger in her voice than she had intended.

"Party pooper!" bawled Sammy. "Party smasher!"

"Tomorrow's better," said Vicki, making a conscious effort to be friendly. "If we plan it today, you can each invite a friend."

"But Mama said we could!" yelled Billy.

"Party! Party!" piped Jill dragging paper plates and napkins out of the cupboard.

"It won't be a real party without friends," reasoned

27

Vicki. "Today, let's take a walk. Each one can invite one person."

"I don't want to walk," said Sammy. "I want a party!"

The walls were closing in. Vicki thought if she didn't get out of the apartment soon, she just might scream.

"Come on," she said firmly. "We'll buy some balloons, and we'll see your friends, and tomorrow, we'll have the party. I promise!"

Grudgingly, the children agreed. Vicki hustled them into their sweaters and out the door. On the steps she stopped and took a deep breath. The fresh air was good in her lungs. The bright sunshine lifted her spirits.

They started down the sidewalk, Jill holding tightly to Vicki's hand. They stopped at the drug store, bought the balloons, and continued on.

At the corner of Pacific and Washington Streets, Vicki saw the entrance to the pier. She sighed. She hadn't planned to come this way. She didn't want to be near the sea today either.

"Hey," said Sammy. "There's the beach!"

He took off in the direction of the pier. Vicki and the others followed, past the shops and cafes, past the gate at the entrance to the beach, and onto the warm sand.

"Last one to the swings is a jellyfish," yelled Sammy, still in the lead.

Vicki stood in the soft sand watching the children cavorting on the swings and tried not to notice the dazzling sea. In spite of her efforts, she looked again and again at the blue water. She saw Zeek's red cap at the end of the pier. Maybe she should go out and just say hello. She hadn't seen Zeek for nearly a week, not since he dropped her down to the *White Star*.

She left the children playing on the swings and wandered down the concrete pier. Zeek was fishing as usual, but he saw her coming.

"Well," he said grinning. "Thought the sharks had you for sure!"

"Not me!" she said glancing toward the marina. No sabots were in sight.

"Where you been?" he asked, a note of worry in his voice.

"Working," she began.

Just then Billy came up with Jill and Sammy right behind. They had followed her onto the pier.

Zeek looked down at the three kids and back at Vicki.

"Yup," said Vicki. "They're mine . . . every afternoon until five o'clock."

"Cramps your style a little, don't it," said Zeek.

"A little," agreed Vicki. "The sabots are meeting today. I told Bob I'd come, only . . ."

"Wait a minute!" said Zeek eyeing her skeptically. "What you got in your head?"

She hadn't had anything in her head when she began, but now an idea was forming. "Nothing," she said.

She watched the kids playing with the boat crane gadgets and talking with the other fishermen. They were fascinated by the bait and the lures and the live fish flopping in the buckets.

She looked out at the horizon. It was full of big sails this afternoon. Every large yacht in the marina must be out today. Only the sabots were missing.

"I did tell him I'd be there," she said wistfully.

"Don't fret about it!" said Zeek.

"Zeek?"

He read her thoughts and shook his head.

"They'll be okay," she said nodding toward the kids. Zeek eyed her skeptically and shook his head.

She continued. "I'd just be a second. I just want to tell Bob I can't come."

"Your mama would fry me in oil if she . . ."

"Oh, but this time she wouldn't know. Nobody would. I'll be back so fast the kids won't even know I'm gone. Besides, I don't have a boat. You need a boat to join the class. Please, Zeek . . ."

He raised his hand to stem the flood. "Okay," he said. "I'm a sucker! But okay!"

She grinned and raced off down the pier toward the marina. She had no bike today, so she'd have to move.

When she reached the dock, she saw the sabot sails, their wooden shoe emblems blazing in the sunshine. They were practicing starts in front of the dock between two red flag marks. Bob was standing on the dock with a bull horn shouting instructions.

Breathlessly, she came up beside him and stood a moment watching the boats. Then she touched his sleeve. He turned, and his face showed surprise and pleasure at the sight of her.

"Hey, sailor!" he exclaimed. "Where you been?"

"I . . ." she was gasping for breath. "I just came to . . ."

"Number fifty-five's free. Want to try?"

It happened so fast Vicki didn't have time to think of the consequences.

"Joe's not coming today," he said. "Come on."

She looked at Joe's little boat with the big 55 on the sail. What could it hurt? Just for a minute!

Bob motioned for her to get in. Then he cast her off.

"Sail it around the first mark and back," he ordered.

She grabbed the tiller and the sheet, the line that held the sail. As she pulled it in, she felt the boat move forward. What next, she thought and tried to remember what she had learned.

Following Bob's directions on the bull horn, she maneuvered the little boat toward the mark.

"Now," he said. "Come about!"

She pushed the tiller away and felt the bow of the boat come up into the wind. The sail began to shake.

"Hold it over," yelled Bob.

She did, and the bow and boom swung over.

"Now," he yelled. "Shift your weight and centerline your tiller!"

She obeyed his commands, and the boat obeyed hers.

"Right!" called Bob. "Now sheet out the sail gradually and bring it back to dock."

She let out the sail turning until she was headed straight for the dock. She was doing it. She was actually sailing the sabot.

Suddenly, she was aware of one important fact. There are no brakes on a sailboat. The dock was dead ahead. She was going to crash!

"Move the helm to starboard! Quick!" Bob's voice was loud in her ear.

Starboard? Which way was . . .

"To the right, Vicki! Now!"

Panic seized her. Mindlessly she obeyed, and the sabot responded just in time, grazing the dock as it passed.

"Okay. Try it again," called Bob.

This time he talked her in and she landed the boat into the wind, letting the wind slow the boat as it approached the dock.

Before she could say anything, he shoved her off.

"Now," he yelled. "Go learn to sail!"

She was off again, breathless and shaking. What little knowledge she had was an unusable knot in her brain.

The boat heeled crazily, the sail only inches from the water. She struggled for control.

"Sheet out!" called Bob. "Ease your sail!"

Instead of easing it, she released it altogether and the sail came up hard. The boat rocked wildly and the bow swung into the wind.

She sat there shaking, drifting backward, "in irons." This was not as easy as it looked!

Gritting her teeth, she slowly tightened the sail and pulled the tiller toward her. The sail began to fill. The boat moved forward. There was a red flag mark ahead. Maybe she could round it.

Back and forth she sailed—tacking, reaching, running. Losing momentum, gaining it again. Heeling over, righting, nearly capsizing a dozen times.

Time got lost somewhere between Bob's voice from the dock and the distant horizon. Perhaps it hid itself among the red flag marks and the twelve white sails. Frightening as it was, she reveled in every wind-blown moment.

Then she heard Bob's voice calling her sail number.

When she was safely back at the dock, he said briskly, "Come on. Let's make it official."

"After that? I was awful!"

"What'd you expect?" he said and started down the dock.

Vicki's head was full of sea air and nothing else as she followed Bob's tall form into the boat house.

"Hang on a minute," he said and went into the inner office.

Vicki looked around. In the corner of the big room on a platform was an old sabot. She walked around it, touching its battered hull. It was like the one she'd been sailing, only it was made of wood, not fiberglas. It's daggerboard was peeling. It's mast was peeling. It's tiller was peeling.

Bob came back with a clipboard, and together they completed the form. Then Vicki signed her name and gave him the seven dollars she'd been saving. Bob handed her the membership card.

"Here it is," he said, "but no formal racing—no regattas—until you get a boat. Understand?"

Vicki nodded. "I don't care about racing," she said.

"You will," he said eyes twinkling.

"Bob?" she said cautiously. "Whose boat is that?"

"Mine," he said.

"Why's it here?"

"Demo. Naming parts. That kind of thing. It's not sea worthy anymore."

"Why not?"

"Leaks all over."

"Can it be fixed?" she asked.

"Sure, but it would cost more to have it fixed than to buy a new one."

"But . . . if somebody wanted it . . ."

Bob looked at her closely. "It's not for sale. I built that thing myself, years ago." He paused and scratched his beard. "In fact, it was my first boat."

"You mean it just sits here? Out of the water?"

Vicki was sheilding her eyes from the sun, which had lowered and was now streaming in the boathouse window.

"Yeah," he said. "What else?"

"What if somebody *wanted* to fix it up?"

"That'd take real dedication. Hours and hours of dedication," he said.

"Bob, I'd be willing to do it. I'd be . . ." Suddenly she realized that the sun in her eyes was tipping the line of fog that grew on the horizon in the evening. *It was evening!*

The kids! The pier! What was she thinking of?

"Bob, I gotta go!" she said, edging toward the door. Then she hesitated. "About the boat. I could do it. Think about it. Will you?"

Without waiting for his answer, she turned and ran.

five

ᖇ Mrs. Baker met them at the door of the apartment, her face a map of worry and irritation. "It's past six!" she said. "What happened?"

"We been to the pier," shouted Billy.

"Yeah," said Sammy.

The kids were out of breath. Vicki had really hustled them home. Mrs. Baker looked at Vicki.

"I'm sorry," said Vicki. "The time got away."

"I caught a fish," piped Jill. She sniffed and wiped her nose on the sleeve of her sweater. "See?"

Triumphantly, from behind her back, she pulled a small perch hanging limply from a piece of fishing line. She sneezed, and the fish fell on the rug.

"Jill!" said her mother, recoiling from the slimy offering. "Put it in the kitchen sink!"

"Can we cook it? Tonight?" asked Jill.

"We'll see. Now move!" Mrs. Baker patted her daughter's bottom as she passed on her way to the kitchen.

"After Vicki left," announced Billy, "Zeek let us ride the boat crane."

"Yeah," shouted Sammy. "Boy, was that fun!"

"Vicki left?" Mrs. Baker turned to Vicki in disbelief. "You left them down there?"

"Zeek was there. He said he'd . . ."

"*You* were in charge." The worry in Mrs. Baker's face had turned to anger.

"I'm sorry," said Vicki, her voice trembling. "I only meant to be gone a minute."

"How long *were* you gone?"

"Well . . . not very . . ."

Billy and Sammy, now aware of the conflict, tried to help.

"It was great," defended Sammy. "Can we go again?"

Jill came back in from the kitchen, her face flushed, her eyes watering.

"And just look at that child!" said Mrs. Baker. "She's sick!" She turned to the kids. "Go wash your hands and face," she commanded.

Under protest they left the room. At the door, Billy turned.

"Can we still have the party tomorrow?" he asked. "We got the balloons!"

"Sure," said Vicki. "I promised."

Now Mrs. Baker turned her full attention to Vicki. "I see no excuse for this," she said coldly.

Vicki nodded miserably. "It's all my fault. I'll stay home from school tomorrow . . . take care of Jill."

"No! They could have drowned . . . or . . . no telling what!"

There was no use trying to explain about Zeek and about the sailing. Vicki was in the wrong.

"I ought to call your mother," said Mrs. Baker.

Vicki's heart skipped a beat. "Please! I won't do it again. Tomorrow, I'll . . ."

"No tomorrows," said Mrs. Baker. "I can't afford them."

Vicki's courage returned. "I understand," she said quietly, "and I'm truly sorry."

The woman's eyes softened a little. "Just thank goodness nobody was hurt." Mrs. Baker paused and shook her head. "Good-bye, Vicki. I'm sorry it didn't work out." She turned and went into the kitchen.

Vicki let herself out of the apartment and started toward home. Mrs. Baker was right. She had been irresponsible. She deserved to be fired. But how was she going to break the news to her mother?

When she came in the door of her own apartment, she found her mother at the sink.

"Hi," said Vicki tentatively.

"Hi," said Sarah.

"Tired?" asked Vicki.

"A little. How was your day?"

"Not bad," Vicki lied. She put down her books and came to where her mother was standing. "Let me do that," she said indicating the potato in the sink. "You go take your bath."

Sarah gave her a grateful smile and handed her the peeler. "My back does hurt," she said and went to get her robe.

Vicki took up the task. Her mother's good mood was a surprise. If she told her now about losing her job, it would dissolve. Would it hurt not to tell for awhile? Tonight she was glad they had no phone.

She finished the potatoes and put the chicken in the pot. Then she set the table. Was it only this afternoon that she had sailed the little boat around the marks? It seemed like much more.

Vicki had dinner ready when her mother came out of the bath. She looked refreshed, and some of the tiredness was gone from around her eyes.

"Soup's on," said Vicki lightly. She ladled the chicken into the bowls, and they sat down together.

"Vicki," said her mother seriously, "I've been thinking. You've got to learn a good trade. Have you given any thought to what you want to do?"

Vicki groped for the right answer, something that would reassure her mother.

"Well . . . I . . ."

Sarah continued. "I've spent my whole life leaning over one conveyor belt or another putting together parts of things—just things—I don't even know what!"

She paused and spread her hands on the table. "And look at these."

Vicki didn't have to look. She knew what her mother's hands looked like. They were nicked and callused. The skin was rough, and the fingers and nails were ingrained with dirt that no amount of scrubbing could erase.

"It's no disgrace, I suppose," said Sarah, "but it's sure no fun. Believe me."

"Maybe you could do something else?" said Vicki.

"I don't know anything else. If only I hadn't . . . If only I'd stayed in school."

"I thought maybe I'd study . . ." Vicki cast wildly about for a finish to her sentence, "uh . . . uh . . . nursing," she blurted.

Her mother's face broke into a smile. "Now you're thinking! People get sick regardless, and the pay is good!"

Vicki squirmed. She knew that nursing required science. Science was her worst subject. Why had she said that!

Sarah's enthusiasm grew. "What made you decide on nursing?"

"I . . . I like to help people," said Vicki lamely. What a dumb answer for her to give, but her mother didn't seem to notice.

"You know you'll have to study and save your money," said Sarah. "I'll help. All I can!"

Vicki nodded. What a can of worms this was going to be.

Sarah snapped her fingers to punctuate a new idea. "I know!" she said. "Your Uncle Joe, the one in Arizona? He owns a health resort. We could save our money, and this summer maybe we'll go! Huh? How about that?" Sarah's face beamed.

"Yeah," said Vicki mustering as much enthusiasm as she could. "That sounds fine."

"We could work for him. Vicki, we could stay!" Caught up with the idea, Sarah went on breathlessly. "Tell you what. Let's try to put your money away, not use it for anything. By summer we'll have enough for the bus tickets!"

"Sure, Mom. That'll be great—just great," said Vicki.

Arizona? Arizona was a desert! She started to get up and clear the table, but her mother put a detaining hand over hers.

"Vicki, I'm so glad you've given up this foolishness about sailing."

Not that, thought Vicki. Not now.

"I understand. I really do," Sarah went on, unaware of her daughter's discomfort. "But it really wouldn't get you anywhere."

"I know," said Vicki shortly. She just couldn't handle that conversation right now.

"I remember when I was your age," continued Sarah. "I wanted to figure skate. I went to the rink every day, watched the skaters all filmy and white in their costumes. It seemed like the most exciting thing in the world." She paused and looked steadily at her daughter. "Vicki, I do understand."

Vicki felt irritation rise in the back of her throat. "It's okay," she said. "I don't have time now anyway."

"That's right. You're going to have to study—especially that science. If you're going to be a nurse . . ."

"If I'm going to be a nurse, I better get started with my homework," Vicki cut in.

"Right," said her mother. She stood up and came around the table to where Vicki was sitting and hugged her daughter. "I'll do the dishes. You get started."

Vicki sat still trying to swallow the large lump of

guilt in her throat. Her mother began clearing the table, humming as she worked.

"Mother," she said.

Sarah turned from the sink and smiled. "What, honey?"

Vicki looked at her mother's face. She hadn't seen her this happy in years.

"Uh . . . nothing."

"What is it?"

"I . . . I was just wondering. What time is it?"

Sarah looked at the kitchen clock. "Eight o'clock," she said. "Better get busy."

Vicki got up from the table and found her science book. She opened the book and began to read, but the ink on the page made her dizzy. She tried to clear her throat, but the lump wouldn't go away.

six

❧ The next afternoon, Vicki sat in the living room of the Ito home. It was furnished Japanese style with grass mats, low black tables, bright pillows, and a large white and black shoji panel in front of the kitchen doorway. The room smelled of ginger and of something good simmering in the kitchen.

Across from her on a pillow sat Tak's mother, a small Japanese lady with a warm smile. They were sipping green tea from small cups with no handles. Vicki was trying to be as graceful on her pillow as Mrs. Ito was on hers. It wasn't easy.

"I'm so glad to meet Takashi's good friend," said Mrs. Ito with only a hint of an accent. "I've heard so many good things about Vicki."

Vicki smiled, charmed by the gentleness of the woman's voice. Tak's voice had the same gentle ring.

"I've wanted to meet you too," said Vicki. "Tak . . . Takashi says you might need someone to look after the twins."

"Ah! Yes!" said Mrs. Ito, her voice lilting. "I have been away from my job for two weeks. I must go back soon."

Vicki knew that Mrs. Ito worked at a school for Japanese children during the late afternoons and on Saturdays. She taught courses, such as the Japanese language, that were not available in American schools. Tak's father was in Japan visiting his own venerable father who, at the age of eighty-five, was gravely ill. It was not known when he would be able to return. He would stay as long as he was needed.

Mrs. Ito poured a second cup of tea. "You would like to look after my children?" she asked.

"Very much," said Vicki.

"And can you come everyday?"

"Everyday but Wednesdays," said Tak emerging from behind the shoji panel with a large sandwich in his hand.

"Oh?" said his mother looking up at her tall son. "And what will . . ."

"Vicki has a sailing class," said Tak. "I'll watch 'em on Wednesdays."

Mrs. Ito looked at Vicki. "Is this right?"

Vicki nodded. "Takashi offered. It's really not necessary if . . ."

"Yes it is," said Tak. "Besides, it's only for a few weeks. Mr. Burns doesn't care as long as I have the boat ready by Friday afternoon."

His mother nodded. "It's settled then?"

Vicki grinned. "It's settled."

"Then perhaps you would like to meet the children?" said Mrs. Ito and gracefully unfolded upward into a standing position. Vicki hoped she could do the same when her turn came. The grass mat was biting into her ankle and the calves of her legs were cramped.

Mrs. Ito excused herself and left the room in search of the twins. Tak came over and offered her his hand. Gratefully she took it, and he pulled her to a standing position. Her legs buckled, but he caught her laughing.

"Take's getting used to," he said.

"How does she do it!" asked Vicki, her feet tingling from having been sat on.

"Easy," he said. "She thinks American, but she still lives Japanese."

Then Mrs. Ito came back into the room with the twins, a pair of seven year old little girls, petite and doll-like even in dungarees. They eyed Vicki with caution.

"This is Misao," she said nodding toward the twin nearest the door. "And this is Kimiko."

Both children smiled shyly.

"Hi," said Vicki brightly.

"Children, this is Vicki, your brother's friend. She will care for you after school each day."

Both children nodded solemnly. Then Misao asked shyly, "Do you like to paint?"

"I do," said Vicki. "Very much. Do you like to play blind man's bluff?"

Both children looked puzzled.

"What's that?" asked Kimiko.

Vicki smiled. "It's a game. I'll teach you." She looked at Mrs. Ito. "Maybe tomorrow?"

"Tomorrow is wonderful!" said Mrs. Ito. "I will call the school and tell them I'll be back."

"I'll show Vicki around," volunteered Tak.

Mrs. Ito left the room, and Tak offered Vicki his arm.

"One guided tour coming up," he said. "First, the yard."

The Ito home was on the canals, an area a quarter of a mile square, fashioned after canals in Venice, Italy. It had never been as grand as that Italian city with its broad waterways and gondolas, yet even in its present need of fresh paint and repairs, this canal area was still the nicest spot in Venice.

Tak opened the door, and Vicki stepped out onto the shaded porch. She had never been here before, and she stood looking at the street of quiet water and at the white wooden foot bridge which arched the canal a few houses down. In spite of the general disrepair of the neighborhood and the broken cars scattered about, it was peaceful. How different from the cramped, noisy apartment building where Vicki and her mother lived.

"It's beautiful," she said softly.

Tak touched her arm. "Come on," he said. "There's more."

They started down the steps and across the lawn toward the canal.

"Your mother is super," said Vicki.

"Yeah," said Tak, "but watch out for those twins."

"But they seem so . . ."

"I know, but don't let their looks fool you," he said grinning. "Once they get to know you . . ."

"I'll try to manage," she said.

"And there's something else," he said, his tone indicating grave danger. "There's snack time."

She looked at him questioningly. "Snack time? What . . ."

"Yes." he said. "The frig. Inside its innocent white door lurks the unknown, the strange, the mysterious." He paused, eyes twinkling. "It's a region not to be entered by the faint of heart."

"Ah," she breathed, taking up his game. "I know. An octopus lurks there just waiting to hug me to death!"

"Right!" he said. "But he's the friendly one. Wait until you meet the raw squid!"

In mock bravado, Vicki drew herself together. "I'll try to be brave," she said. Then she laughed and squeezed his hand. "It'll be such fun!"

"Yeah," he said looking steadily into her eyes. "Yeah!"

She felt her cheeks burning and looked back toward the water. A small row boat was tied to the dock next door.

"Can you sail on the canals?" she asked.

"Not any more," he said. "Now they're too shallow. The people that lived here used to though. That's why our garage is like it is."

Vicki looked back toward the garage part of the house and saw for the first time a high sloping roof, a large car-sized door, and what looked like a driveway leading down to the canal.

"For boats?"

He nodded. "I'll show you."

He took her through the garage, opening and closing the doors as they went. They came out of the garage into the carport on the street side and went back into the house.

Mrs. Ito was waiting with a key and all manner of instructions and emergency numbers. She ended by inviting Vicki to stay for dinner.

Vicki declined, explaining that her mother would be expecting her.

"You better stay," said Tak. "It's safe tonight."

"Safe?" asked Vicki looking at Mrs. Ito.

"Yeah," said Tak. It's *dashi*, Japanese soup. Everything's cooked."

Vicki laughed and took Mrs. Ito's hand. "Thank you so much for inviting me. Another time, I'd love to stay," she said.

Tak walked her home through the twilight. They talked of the twins and the sailing class and his job on the boat—nice things, easy things. Vicki let the relief of having found a job and the pleasure of working at Tak's house wash over her. Surely her mother wouldn't be too upset now that she had another job.

Tak left her at the door of the apartment, and she went in. She found her mother mending her yellow sweater and looking relaxed, last night's good humor still upon her.

"You worked late tonight," said Sarah.

"Not exactly," said Vicki. Then she told about losing the job at the Baker house—not all of it—only that Mrs. Baker no longer needed her.

Sarah wanted to know why, but Vicki rushed ahead with the news that the new job was at twice the salary and that the Ito twins were absolutely adorable.

"Ito?" asked Sarah. "You mean that nice young man?"

Vicki grinned. "Tak." she said. "They're his sisters."

Her mother had met Tak several times when he had walked her home, and she had liked him immediately.

"You'll like his mother too," said Vicki. "She's great."

"Vicki, I'm delighted," said Sarah, "and how lucky for us that they need someone to look after the twins."

Her mother seemed genuinely pleased.

Vicki was relieved. She had neglected to mention about leaving the Baker children on the pier and about the sailing class. She had neglected to mention that she fully intended to continue with the class. She had neglected to mention that in the back of her mind was a hope . . . a hope which took the shape of a battered and peeling hull.

"Number Seventeen! Trim that sail!" came Bob's voice on the bull horn. Vicki was in Twenty-Nine, its owner being housebound with the flu. It was the last class of the season. The sabots were really moving today —except for Seventeen, which could never find the wind.

The breeze was fresher than usual. Two of the boys had already capsized, righted, bailed out their boats and gone in for dry clothes. Now they were in a practice race, a basic part of all sailing classes which helped sharpen and refine sailing skills. Vicki and two of the boys were in the lead. Number Seventeen was beating only his own stern.

Her boat and the other two neared the final mark,

running before the wind. Vicki was in third place. If she could get on the inside, she just might have a chance.

The bow of her boat was coming up on the sabot in front of her. There. Now it overlapped!

"Room at the mark!" she called. The boy in front of her swore and eased his boat away. She'd done it. She was on the inside.

The mark was dead ahead. As she approached it she lowered the daggerboard and sheeted in her sail. Then she pushed the tiller hard away and came around the mark full up on the wind.

Now she, Vicki Banyon, novice of the class, was in the lead. If she maintained it, she would win!

"Good girl, Vicki!" came Bob's voice clear and strong.

The boat heeled fiercely, and Vicki threw her weight to the high side, hiking out over the edge of the boat as far as she dared. Then a sudden gust hit the sail and pushed the little boat on over. *Capsize!*

Vicki tried to go over the high side of the boat, but her foot slipped, and she fell into the icy water. She knew what to do. As she swam around toward the stern of the boat, the two sabots she had beaten out at the mark passed by.

"How dry I am. How dry I am!" sang the first skipper as he passed.

"Next time, take a bus!" yelled the second. Not so musical, but equally deflating.

Vicki laughed in spite of her predicament. Capsizes happened in the small boats, and they all knew it.

She righted the boat and began bailing furiously.

49

Vicki threw her weight to the high side,
hiking out over the edge of the boat as far as she dared.

When she had enough water out of the boat, she climbed in, finished the bailing and continued the race. All of the other sabots, even Number Seventeen, had crossed the finish line ahead of her. Last, she thought, her teeth chattering, but there. Not to finish was the only true disgrace. ~~END~~

She docked amid jeers and guffaws from her fellow skippers.

"Just proves *men* make better sailors," said one thumping his chest Tarzan style.

"Yeah," said another. "Girl's are better cooks. Too bad we don't have galleys."

"What's she doin' here anyway," whined the Number Seventeen skipper. "She doesn't even have a boat."

Vicki had taken all the ribbing good naturedly until the last one. Now her grin dissolved.

Dripping and shivering, she turned toward the boat-house. It was true, of course, she didn't have a boat. Bob had bent the rules to let her join. She had been using the other kids' boats, but only when someone was absent or came in for a rest. She'd never kept any of them from sailing.

Then she heard Bob's voice.

"What do you mean, she doesn't have a boat!"

Vicki stopped short and listened.

"You know the rules," continued Bob. "You have to have a boat to belong here."

"Where is it," demanded one of the sailors she'd almost beaten today. "She always uses ours."

"In dry dock! Come back in March and see for yourself."

Vicki stood still and looked at Bob from the boat house door, her wet clothes and her shivers forgotten. She knew what he meant. She'd been hinting about his wooden boat for weeks.

Bob yelled to her from the dock. "Get yourself dry, kid. I want to talk to you."

"Yes, Sir!" said Vicki and made for the dressing room.

When she came out, dry and warm, the boys had gone. Bob was inspecting the wooden sabot.

"Okay," he said. "You asked for it. How's your supply of dedication!"

Vicki grinned. "I'm loaded!" she said.

"Don't look so happy. You don't know what you're in for."

"I don't care, Bob. I'll do it."

"Got a place to work on it?"

Vicki thought of the big empty garage at the Ito house.

"Yes," she said firmly. She had already discussed the possibility with Tak. She had only to get Mrs. Ito's approval.

"You'll have the winter to fix it up," said Bob. "Most of it's just hard work, sanding, patching, finishing—that kind of thing. There'll be some expense for sand-paper and varnish, but not much."

Vicki nodded solemnly.

Bob continued. "If the boat is ready for the first regatta in March, it's yours."

Vicki stared. "Mine?"

"Right," said Bob. "If you do all that, you'll have earned it!"

Vicki touched the wooden hull. Her boat! She saw it now, as it would be, clean and gleaming.

"When . . . when can I get it?" she asked.

"I'll bring it to you next Wednesday," he said. "Just tell me where."

Vicki wrote the address of the Ito home on a slip of paper and handed it to Bob. "I'll check with Mrs. Ito," she said, "but I'm sure it's okay."

In return he gave her a card with his address and phone number on it.

"Call me if there's a problem," he said. Then he held out his hand. Vicki shook it firmly then pulled him down and kissed his woolly cheek.

"Okay, sailor," he said gruffly. "Now git. I've got things to do."

Vicki's spirits carried her home only inches below the clouds. Nothing could spoil this day. She was going to have a boat, and not just any boat—Bob's boat. After dinner she'd go over to Tak's, talk to Mrs. Ito about using the garage.

When she arrived home and opened the door of her apartment she found her mother sitting at the kitchen table writing a letter.

"What's up?" asked Vicki. "You're home early."

"This." Her mother's face was grim. She handed Vicki a check signed by her employer. "Take a good look. There won't be anymore of them."

Vicki's heart contracted. "But, why?"

"The plant's closing. It's out of business, and I'm out of a job." Sarah's voice was toneless.

"Just like that? No notice? Nothing?"

"Just like that," said her mother.

The two looked at each other for a moment.

"It's happened before," said Vicki hopefully. "You've always found another job."

"Not this time. Jobs are scarce now."

"But . . ."

"Money's tight." Sarah fingered the letter she was writing. "Maybe Joe has room for us. I wanted to wait 'til summer, but now . . ."

Vicki froze inside. Not now! Not Arizona!

"Maybe you'll be lucky," she said. "They'll give you a good recommendation."

Sarah nodded. "They did, but when have I ever been lucky?"

Vicki went to the refrigerator. "We're out of milk," she said. "I'll go get some."

She had to get away.

"Okay," Sarah said absently. She was already back into her letter to Joe.

Vicki let herself quietly out of the apartment. In the hall outside she paused, took a deep breath, and hugged the yellow sweater she was wearing.

seven

The next five days were difficult. Sarah went out each morning job hunting and came home each night aching and disappointed. The little money they had dwindled. Vicki thought of calling Bob and telling him not to bring the boat, but somehow she couldn't.

On Tuesday evening, the night before the sabot was to be delivered, Vicki sat at the kitchen table doing her science homework. She had to do well in science now that she had committed herself. Her mother was counting on it. Maybe today Sarah would be lucky, find a good job. Maybe then she wouldn't be so anxious to go to Arizona. It was too soon to hear from Joe, but Sarah talked about it every day.

Vicki heard the key in the lock and looked up to see her mother standing in the doorway.

"Hi," said Vicki brightly. "Any luck?"

Sarah nodded, but her face didn't register pleasure. "I got a job," she said. "Know what it is?"

Vicki shook her head.

"The 'Round the Clock Answering Service'," said Sarah and sank into a chair.

In spite of her mother's apparent gloom, Vicki's hopes soared. "That's great," she said. "No more assembly line, no more . . ."

"Is it?" cut in Sarah. "It's clear up on Centinela Avenue. The pay's lousy, and would you like to guess which part of the clock I'll be working?"

Vicki's hopes crumpled in her lap. "Nights?" she asked.

Sarah nodded. "Ten at night to six in the morning."

The news couldn't have been worse.

"Are you gonna take it?" Vicki asked softly.

"What choice do I have?"

"The phone company—Mother, I know they . . ."

"I tried. They're not hiring."

Vicki thought of her mother walking the streets of Venice at night on her way to work and again in the early hours of the morning. Aside from the fact that it was at least a two mile walk, it was dangerous!

"I hate it!" said her mother. "You alone in this crumby apartment . . ."

"I'll be okay," said Vicki. In truth, she was a little apprehensive, but her mother didn't need to know that right now.

"Let's get a phone," she ventured.

Her mother stared. "A phone! And just how would you suggest we pay for a phone? We couldn't do it on my last salary."

"Well, maybe I could pay for it out of my salary."

"Don't be silly!"

"But it *would* help," Vicki persisted.

"Sure it would," said Sarah. "So would a nice apartment in one of those maximum security buildings. So would a car! So would a lot of things!"

Vicki felt the sting of her mother's anger. "Mom," she said softly. "Don't take it."

"We have to eat. We have to pay the rent. I start tomorrow night," said Sarah tonelessly.

Vicki nodded. Arizona was only a matter of time. No hungry gulls, no salt air. How would she breathe?

The next afternoon Vicki and Tak stood in the carport of the Ito home waiting for Bob and the sabot. She hadn't called him. She'd gone to the drug store twice last evening, put her dime in and started to dial, but each time something had stopped her. Now, any minute, he'd be here.

She was gambling and the odds were against her. She knew it. But Tak had promised that if she had to leave, he'd see that Bob got the boat back. At least she didn't have to worry about that.

"What about a name?" Tak's voice broke into her thoughts.

"I have one," she said.

Since the first time she saw the little boat standing forlornly in the boathouse, she'd known what its name should be.

"Want to tell me?"

"I can't," she said. "Not yet."

He nodded.

They heard tires on the gravel road and looked up

to see Bob's blue sedan with the sabot strapped to the top making its way along the narrow road. The mast had a red flag tied to the end of it and was sticking out of the car's back window.

They waved, and Bob pulled the car into the carport.

"Whew!" said Bob. "Almost lost the boat on that last bridge."

"Welcome to the canals," said Tak laughing.

"I'd forgotten how it is down here," said Bob.

Vicki introduced Bob and Tak, and the three of them unstrapped the boat from the top of the car. Tak and Bob carried it through the carport and into the garage. Vicki pulled out the mast and followed.

The twins had heard the car arrive and came out of the house.

"Wow!" yelled Kimiko looking at the boat. "It's a mess."

Bob grinned. "Now there's an honest girl."

Vicki laughed. "She's going to help fix it up."

Misao came shyly over to where the group was standing. "I get to help paint," she said.

"Come on," said Vicki to the twins. "Right now you can help carry the rest of the stuff back." She took the twins to the car and loaded them down with the tiller, daggerboard and the like. When they came back Bob and Tak had the boat positioned, bottom up, on a pair of sawhorses.

"How's your sanding arm?" Bob asked Kimiko.

The little girl flexed her muscle. "Good," she said admiring the small bulge in the sleeve of her shirt. "Can we start, Vicki?"

They heard tires on the gravel road and looked up to see
Bob's blue sedan with the sabot strapped to the top.

Bob grinned. "Eager crew you have!"

"Right," said Vicki.

"One thing," said Bob. "It doesn't have a sail. I forgot that the old one was worn out. I brought it, but it's worthless, can't even be mended."

Vicki gulped. She didn't know how she was going to buy sandpaper, let alone a *sail*.

"How . . . how much do you think one would cost?" She tried not to sound worried.

"New? Maybe fifty."

Tak whistled. "That much?"

"Yeah, but you could always make one. That's why I brought the old one. If you can find an old sail from a big boat, you can use the good parts. Sometimes the sailmaker gets them in, sell them for patches. Better still, buy the new fabric and make one out of that."

"Don't worry about it," said Vicki, more courage in her voice than she felt.

Bob looked at his watch. "Better run," he said. "Sandy's waiting dinner." He paused. "By the way, she sent you a kiss." He leaned over and delivered the present. "Good luck, sailor. Call me if you need me."

"I will," said Vicki. "And Bob . . . thanks for everything!"

Waving aside her gratitude, Bob climbed into his car and drove away down the narrow road.

Tak and Vicki and the twins turned back to the object of interest in the garage. Tak raised the door on the canal side to let in the evening light. Then the four of them walked around the eight foot hull, talking about the work that was to be done, how they would do it, and what they needed to buy.

Kimiko had been right. It was a mess. First, it needed sanding to get off all the peeling paint and varnish. That would be a big job requiring at least three grades of sandpaper—coarse, medium, and fine.

The twins, bored by the technical aspects of the project, went off to find a snack in the mysterious regions of their mother's "frig." Tak went in search of some sandpaper.

Vicki stood looking at the boat. Then she laid both her palms on the boat's hull and closed her eyes. Silently, she resolved to bring whatever energy, whatever love, whatever dedication was needed to make it whole again. Maybe big dreams did end in heartbreak, but this one was growing warm under her hands. If it was within her power, she would see it finished, launched . . . .

She felt two equally warm hands cover her own on the hull of the small boat. She felt Tak's cheek, soft against her hair, and the warmth of his body behind her.

"Hey lady," he said.

She turned and looked into his face.

"Hey lady, there's a sunrise on your forehead," he said. Then he bent his head and touched her lips with his own.

"What . . . what's happening . . ." she said at last.

"Simple," he said. "We love . . . the sea . . . this leaky old boat . . . and each other."

His arms closed around her, and for a moment there was nothing else in the world that mattered but this.

A giggle from Kimiko, standing at the garage entrance, jarred the moment.

"Scram, brat!" yelled Tak hoarsely picking up a stray tennis ball and hurling it in her direction. The twin disappeared, and they looked at each other again.

"Beginnings," said Vicki looking at the boat.

"Yeah. That's where it is," he said looking at her.

eight

∾ The thing Vicki hated most about the new schedule was waking up on dark, foggy mornings to an empty apartment. Now, shivering in her sweater and jeans, she glanced nervously at the kitchen clock. It was almost eight. Her mother was late. In the two weeks since Sarah had started the new job, she had never been this late.

The teakettle whistled from the stove, and Vicki poured herself a cup of instant cocoa. If her mother didn't come soon, she'd have to go on. School started in half an hour.

So far there had been no word from Uncle Joe, but her mother watched the mail each day. Sarah hated this night job. She found it hard to sleep during the day, and she worried constantly about Vicki being alone.

A knock came at the door. Vicki wondered who it could be.

The knock came again, more urgent this time. Vicki went cautiously to the door.

"Who's there?" she called.

"It's me. Let me in!" It was her mother's voice all right, but strange, almost sobbing.

Quickly, Vicki released the night latch and opened the door. Sarah stood in the hall, her hair a mess, dried blood under her nose. A large puffy bruise was growing around one eye. She all but fell into Vicki's arms.

Vicki helped her to the sofa and ran to get a wet towel.

"Wha . . . what happened?" she cried.

"My purse!" sobbed Sarah. "A man came out of an alley and grabbed my purse. Oh Vicki! I cashed my paycheck yesterday. All of it was in that purse!

Vicki carefully wiped her mother's face. "But how did you get hurt?"

"I . . . I tried to get it back, but he . . . he . . ."

"Never mind," said Vicki. "You're lucky he didn't kill you."

The eye was closing fast. Vicki knew she had to do something.

"Hold still," she commanded. "I'll get an ice pack."

She ran to the refrigerator and began wrestling the ice cubes out of the tray.

"Have you told the police?" she called from the kitchen.

"No," said Sarah. "What could they do?"

Vicki came back with a towel full of ice and placed it gently on the swelling eye. "I'll call them."

"But, it was dark. I didn't see his face."

"It's okay. I'll call them anyway."

"No. You go on to school," said her mother steadying the ice pack on her face. "It must be late. I felt shaky, dizzy, so I stopped at an all night diner for a while . . ."

"I'm staying home today," said Vicki firmly. "You need . . ."

"I'm okay now," said Sarah lying back against the pillows.

"You need a doctor," said Vicki.

"I'll be all right." Sarah raised herself to a sitting position. "Nothing is going to get in the way of your school. *Nothing*!"

Vicki sighed. "Okay," she agreed, "but first I'll fix you some breakfast."

"No. You go now!" Sarah lay back on the pillows and closed her eyes. Vicki covered her with a blanket and bent to kiss her cheek.

"I'm so sorry," she whispered.

"It's not your fault, honey," said her mother without opening her eyes.

Vicki let herself out of the apartment, setting the night latch as she went. Maybe it wasn't her fault, but she felt as if it were, at least partly. She had to do something!

She stopped at the drug store near the school and went into the phone booth just outside the door. She called the police station and reported the attack and the theft. Then she called the telephone company. *Enb*

Three days later, Vicki and the twins were busy in the Ito garage. Vicki was sanding hard and thinking hard. The police had been at the house yesterday and taken Sarah's statement, but they didn't give much hope of finding the thief. There was almost no hope at all of getting the purse back. They had cautioned Mrs.

Banyon about being out at *that* time of night in *that* neighborhood, but what could her mother do? There were no buses running.

Kimiko's eager voice broke her thoughts. "Is that good enough?"

Vicki stopped her own work and came over to run her hand on the smoothly sanded surface.

"That's fine, Kimmy," she assured her. "Look at that wood!" The grain was beginning to show. "Wait 'til that's varnished!"

"Are we almost done?" asked Kimiko.

"Almost," said Vicki. "If we hustle, we can finish the sanding today."

"Then can we paint?" asked Misao from the other side of the boat. Misao had been ready to paint since the first day.

"Not yet," said Vicki. "Tomorrow I'll get some patch. We have to fill the holes so it won't leak."

"Won't we *ever* paint?" asked Misao, then looking over Vicki's shoulder toward the lawn and the canal, Misao said, "Hi, Mr. Johnson."

Vicki turned to see a slender young man standing in the middle of the lawn watching them. As she looked up, he came toward them.

"Quite a project," he said.

"Yeah," said Misao. "We're almost done sanding!"

"Not quite," said Vicki thinking of the mast and the daggerboard and the rudder still standing against the garage wall untouched. "Just the hull so far."

"Lotta work for this old tub," he said.

Vicki felt irritation at the word *tub*, but she said nothing.

"Whatcha gonna do when you're done? Sell it?"

"No," said Vicki a little sharply. "We'll sail it!"

"Be worth quite a bit," he said. "Good wood. I might want it."

"I'm sorry," said Vicki shortly. "It's not for sale."

The man shrugged. "If you change your mind, let me know."

He sauntered off in the direction of the house next door.

"Who's that?" asked Vicki.

"Man who visits next door sometimes," said Misao.

"Yeah," said Kimiko. "He's weird."

Vicki felt a twinge of uneasiness, but dismissed it.

"Hey, gang!" It was Tak coming toward the garage at a gallop. He was early today. Usually he didn't get home until after six.

"Hi," said Vicki. Her spirits always rose when he arrived.

"Guess what I've got, and you can have it!" he said to his audience of three. One hand was held tightly behind his back.

Misao guessed popsicles and Kimiko guessed a package of bubble gum. Tak often brought goodies for the twins. Both were wrong.

Tak nodded at Vicki. "Your turn," he said, eyes twinkling.

Vicki shrugged. "A three-sided lop eater?" she suggested. "It's just what we've been needing."

"Very good," exclaimed Tak, "but very wrong. Guess again."

"A string-fed sea cobbler?" said Vicki. "We don't have one of those either."

Tak shook his head. "Another fine idea, but still wrong. You give?"

All nodded.

From behind his back he brought a flat, round can. The twins looked disappointed, but Vicki squealed, leaped up, and planted a kiss on his cheek.

"Patch!" she cried. "Where did you find patch!"

"Mr. Burns used it last weekend on the yacht. It would only stand around and get hard, so he gave it to me."

Vicki took the can and opened it. It had been opened before and a little taken out, but it was a new can. She looked at Tak. He was capable of buying it with his own money and then fixing it so Vicki wouldn't know.

"Come on," said Tak. "Let's see if it works."

It was almost time for her to leave. "Wait," she said. "I'll call home. Then Mother won't worry."

Now it was Tak's turn to look at Vicki.

"Phone?" he asked.

She nodded, trying to manage a nonchalant smile.

"Your sail money," he said.

She shrugged. "After what happened to my mother, we had to have it."

Tak nodded.

"Back in a minute," she yelled and went toward the house.

That afternoon they finished the sanding and did all of the big patches. With Tak's help, the work went fast. It was Friday. The patch would have the weekend to dry.

When they finished it was nearly seven-thirty. Mrs. Ito was home now and had a pot of *dashi* on the stove. She invited Vicki to dinner. This time Vicki accepted.

During dinner they talked about the progress of the boat. Vicki hoped that soon they'd be able to put it in the canal and test it for leaks.

After dinner, Tak walked her home. When they reached the steps of her apartment, she invited him in for hot chocolate.

"But remember," she said as they started up the stairs, "there is something Mother doesn't know about."

He grinned.

"What boat?" he said. "Who has a boat?"

Their eyes met, and a look of understanding passed between them. Then they continued up the stairs.

The sailmaker spread the new sail on the counter. Vicki and the twins looked wide-eyed. Crisp white dacron with a red wooden shoe emblem near the top!

"No charge for the numbers," he said.

"Well . . . uh, I don't have the money right now," said Vicki, "but how much is it . . . all together?"

"Forty-nine dollars plus tax . . . fifty-one, ninety-four," he said briskly.

Vicki paused then asked. "Could I just . . . just buy the fabric?"

The sailmaker rubbed his jaw. "Make your own?"

Vicki nodded.

"Know how?"

"No," she said, "But I can learn."

"It's not as easy as it looks," he said. "Got a machine?"

"No."

"Pretty tough," he said. He looked at Vicki carefully, as if assessing her abilities. "I suppose it could be . . ."

"How much just for the material?" she asked. Both Misao and Kimiko had their fingers crossed.

"Let's see . . ." He measured the length of the sail and raised his eyes to the ceiling to calculate. " 'Bout fifteen dollars, and three dollars for the shoe."

That was better, but it was still more than she could save. "What about an old sail . . . a big one?"

He shook his head. "Wouldn't recommend it. Old fabric tears too easy. I use 'em for patches."

"Can it be done?" Vicki persisted.

"Sure. Cost you maybe five dollars for the sail, *if* I have one."

"Do you?"

"Not now, but I may."

Vicki's voice was firm. "Will you call me if you get one in?"

He shrugged. "Sure. Give me your number."

Vicki scribbled the Ito's phone number on a pad, and beside it she wrote her name. Then she thanked him, and they left.

On the way home, Kimiko asked, "Why did you use our phone?"

Vicki winced. "Uh . . . I'm there most of the time," she managed.

"Oh," said Kimiko, satisfied with the answer. Vicki wasn't. She lived these days with a large portion of guilt weighing on her mind and with the fear of discovery around every corner. Maybe when the boat was done, maybe then her mother would understand.

nine

∾ The winter deepened. The holidays came and went. Tak's gift to her was a red wooden shoe emblem for the sail.

"If you get the money for the new sail," he said, "you can put this on a jacket or something." There was little chance of that, and he knew it.

Her gift to him was a pen and ink drawing she had made of him at the helm of a big yacht. "Next year," she told him, "I'll buy you a real present."

"What's real," he had said, "if this isn't."

The twins reported that he had framed the drawing and hung it in his room.

For his birthday, a few weeks later, she gave him a poem she had found about going down to the sea in ships. According to her two spies, he hung it in a matching frame beside the ink drawing.

At last, the boat was beginning to show the effort they were making. The hull was finished, varnished to a high gleam. It was righted now on the sawhorses, and the mast, also newly varnished, was stepped in its proper position in the boat. All the hardware had been oiled and polished. All of it was there, and none of it was broken.

Vicki never came to the garage now without standing a moment and just looking at the little boat. Bob had used teak wood when he built it, and teak never lost its warmth. Now, its grain restored, it was the color of honey stirred once with a spoonful of molasses. The rich smell of fresh varnish hovered in the air.

At present the twins and Vicki were working on the rudder, the piece which, when connected to the tiller, steered the boat. Next would be the daggerboard which fitted into the slot in the center of the boat and kept it on course. Both parts had to be done carefully since they were in the water every time the boat was in use. On Bob's recommendation, they were applying extra coats of varnish on these two parts. It took time, but Vicki was determined to do it right.

The twins had been promised sailing rights and so felt that they were in partnership with Vicki. Misao was content to dream of Vicki taking her out. Kimiko, brave to a fault, wanted to learn to sail, and Vicki had promised to teach her.

Vicki was losing sleep over the sail. She had five dollars tucked away, in case the sailmaker got an old one in, but with the money crunch the way it was, saving any more was out of the question. Regardless, she had to have a sail, even if she had to make one out of an old sail. She'd gotten a book on sailmaking from the library and studied it. She was pretty sure she could do it, and she did have Bob's old one to use as a pattern.

At home, Sarah Banyon had launched a one woman

campaign to make Vicki an "A" student. Vicki had been assigned regular study hours. Her books and lessons were inspected daily. No day passed in which Sarah did not say at least once, "When you're a nurse, you'll never be in the fix I'm in." Vicki obliged as much as she could.

The phone had been a big help. Sarah checked in when she got to work at night so that each knew the other was safe. She called again before she left in the morning to make sure Vicki was up and getting ready for school, and to let Vicki know she was on her way home. They had agreed that if Sarah did not arrive home in one hour, Vicki was to call the police.

Vicki was not really afraid to stay alone at night, but it was comforting to have the telephone at hand with her mother's work number and the Ito number for emergencies.

Then the letter arrived from Joe. He apologized for the delay in answering Sarah's letter. He had been out of town when it arrived, and somehow it had gotten buried under the clutter on his desk. He had only discovered it today.

"By all means come!" he said. "The weather's warm. The sun is bright." He had no job openings until spring, but he had plenty of room for his sister and her daughter.

Sarah was relieved. She too had been tucking money into a sock. As soon as she had enough, they would go. She sat right down to answer Joe's letter.

"We can't go now!" Vicki blurted, sudden desperation driving away reason. Her mother's startled look

Vicki had been assigned regular study hours.

brought her back, and she continued with forced calm. "I can't change schools, especially in the middle of a term!"

"We'll see," her mother had said.

That night Vicki was awake a long time. Conscience told her that Arizona was her mother's chance to rest, but her own need for the sea was overpowering. The two wouldn't mix. She lived two different lives: her own—full of Tak, the twins, the sabot, and the sea—and her mother's world of hope about a nursing career and a promised land which held no promise for her.

Vicki's affection for the Ito family had grown steadily. Tak's warning about the twins had proved to be little more than a joke. True, they were into everything, but they were also loving and eager to please. Their excitement over the wooden sabot was almost as great as her own.

Mrs. Ito was a joy. She loved Vicki and made it plain that she did. She thought fixing the boat was a wonderful way for her children to spend the long winter months. She had said often that they were learning something that they otherwise might not have the chance to learn.

Vicki's only problem with Mrs. Ito was that she wanted to visit Sarah. Not a bad idea, but there was no way for this meeting to take place without Sarah finding out about the boat. What would happen then? Sooner or later, she would have to know, but if it happened now, Vicki was sure that overnight, she would find herself on the desert sands of Arizona. Daily she walked a tight rope, prolonging the visit as long as possible without offending Mrs. Ito.

Three more times Vicki called the sailmaker. Spring was already announcing its intended arrival with occasional warm breezes and the budding of the gardenia bush near the Ito porch. Three times the sailmaker had not had an old sail for her.

What if he didn't get one in? What if she had the boat all done, but no sail? Would all her work, and the twins' and Tak's work be for nothing? Most of all, how could she bear to lose the little boat now. It was almost like a part of her own body. She knew every piece of wood, every bolt and screw, every joint in it better than she knew the configuration of her own face. Its name, as yet unspoken, was already engraved in her mind.

"Maybe next week," the sailmaker had said. She prayed it would be so.

In this time too, she had come to appreciate Tak, not only for his gentleness and his understanding, but for himself. He was not without friends, but as far as Vicki knew, she was his only close friend. She cherished this. Neither of them sought or needed the usual ties that others formed. Tak had explained it once.

"They don't know where I am. I like 'em, but my life's full already."

That was about it. Maybe this wasn't the love everybody raved about. Yet ever since that first morning on the pier, when he had thrown his jacket around her shoulders, they had shared the warmth and pleasure of each other's lives.

Wasn't that enough? Wasn't that more than some who called themselves "in love" had ever found?

ten

~~ "Okay!" said Bob. "Let's see who's done his home-work!" He was standing on the dock near the boat-house with the twelve boys and Vicki. It was a gray February afternoon, and the first class of the new season had begun. They stood shivering in their wind breakers. The twelve sails lined up in front of them rustled in the light, chilly air.

"Four at a time," he ordered. "Out. Around the marks to port, and back. And *try* not to turn over. That water's cold!"

The first four boys took off, climbed into their boats and left the dock. Vicki was standing next to Bob. He spoke to her as he watched the sails.

"How's the boat coming?" He hadn't seen it since he delivered it to her last fall.

"Fine," she said. "It's done. Come see."

"You're kidding!" said Bob in amazement. "The sail too?"

"No," said Vicki, "but I'm working on it." She hesitated a moment. "Can I name it now? I've got a . . ."

"Not until you get the sail."

"Okay," she answered. Bob was right. The boat wasn't really hers yet, and only the owner of a boat had the right and responsibility of giving it a name.

The four sabots were having difficulty. It was obvious that the skippers hadn't given sailing a second thought since the last class in November. As they brought the boats clumsily into the dock, Bob hassled them about forgetting all they'd ever known. Then he nodded at Vicki and three others.

"Get going!" he said, "and try to do it right."

Vicki climbed into the sabot and cast off. She had been studying all winter, keeping her books at Tak's house.

Out she went, and she rounded the first mark with ease. The thrill of sailing again after so many months made her forget the cold.

"That's it, Vicki!" called Bob on the bull horn. Then "Number Seventeen, you're luffing! Sheet in and sail your boat!"

She looked back at Seventeen. His sail was shaking all over, and he was drifting backwards.

Vicki was half a boat length ahead of any of the others. It seemed natural now. All the things she'd learned last fall had come together with her winter study and with her newly acquired knowledge of the boat itself. The one in the Ito garage had made her aware of things she otherwise wouldn't have thought of, like the exact position of the daggerboard in the water and how it kept the boat on course.

Before she knew it, she was back at the dock with Bob grinning broadly down at her.

"Well, kid! You may make a sailor after all." This was high praise from Bob.

She blushed, took his hand, and stepped out of the boat.

The boy waiting to sail the boat gave her an unfriendly stare and got in. Bob shoved him off along with the other four.

"Mr. Schaffer?" said one of the boys who had returned with Vicki, "my little brother wants to learn. Is there a beginning class this year?"

"Not yet," said Bob. "I don't have the time, and I don't have an instructor for it."

A spark went off in Vicki's head. She could do it. She could teach that class!

"I'll teach it for you, Mr. Schaffer," announced Joe, the winning skipper from last year's class.

"We'll see," said Bob.

Vicki knew Joe was good, but he sailed by the seat of his pants. The more Vicki studied, the more she realized that sailing was a sport and a science as well. The more you knew about tides, currents, wind and weather, and the fine points of seamanship, the better. Joe had a good "feel" for sailing, but he relied too heavily upon it. He hadn't bothered to study beyond the basics. Expert skippers, like Bob, had both, and the natural talent coupled with expertise was what made them champions.

The others came back to the dock, and Bob started the sail-offs. The three kids who came in first would sail against each other. Vicki and the other two climbed back into the boats and took off.

Out they went and rounded the first two marks. Then they came downwind toward the final mark, running. Running? All three of them sat motionless in the water, their sails drooping. The other two boats were ahead of Vicki's, but not by much.

There was almost no wind. Vicki knew that the real test of a sailor was how he handled the boat in very light air. Try as she would, she couldn't make the sabot go.

"Anyone for chess?" quipped the boy in the boat just ahead of hers.

"How 'bout Monopoly," said Joe, disgusted. "There's time!" Joe's boat was in the lead, but he was going nowhere.

Then Vicki remembered something she'd read. She eased the tiller to port, and the bow of the boat moved slightly to starboard. Her sail filled, not much, but enough to give her forward motion. Gradually, she overtook the other boats and passed.

"Stop blowing on your sail," yelled Joe as she passed.

Vicki grinned back at him. "Wind is wind," she pointed out.

Back at the dock, Joe grumbled. "Luck! She got our wind."

"Maybe," said Bob. "Let's see how she does against the expert."

He grabbed the first sabot in the row and climbed in. "Come on, Vicki!"

Vicki gasped. Her mind went blank. Race against Bob?

Off they started toward the first mark, Bob in the lead.

She watched him maneuver his sabot and tried to follow his example. She was doing it. Her boat was responding better than it had before, but she couldn't catch Bob. He won by about three boat lengths, and the boys applauded and yelled.

"Whew," he exclaimed as they docked. "I was afraid you'd embarrass me."

After the boats were unrigged, Vicki turned to Bob. "Maybe . . . maybe I could help with the beginning class," she ventured.

Bob grinned. "That's an idea. See me after the first regatta."

"But . . . am I good enough?"

"Right on, sailor, but you don't have any real racing experience."

Vicki felt her pride swell. She thought of the little boat in the Ito garage.

"When's the first regatta?" she asked.

"A week from Saturday," he said. "Better get on that sail."

She nodded. "Don't worry," she said inwardly quaking. How was she going to manage? Old handkerchiefs?

The next afternoon Vicki was fixing the twins a snack when the phone rang in the Ito kitchen. Misao leaped to answer.

"It's for you," she said gravely.

Vicki's heart sank. Maybe something was wrong with her mother. She took the receiver.

"Miss Banyon?" came a gruff male voice on the line.

"Yes?" said Vicki.

"Got a sail for you," said the voice. "Still want it?"

The sailmaker!

"Yes . . . yes I do!" she answered excitedly. "The sail," she mouthed at the two faces on the other side of the counter.

"It's bigger than I thought. I'll have to get seven-fifty for it," he said.

Vicki did some quick arithmetic. She still had the five tucked away and money for the phone bill. She'd ordered the phone after her mother was attacked, and she'd been paying for it ever since.

"Okay," she said. "I'll be right there."

She hung up and turned to the twins. "Let's go!" she commanded.

They scampered for their sweaters.

The next afternoon was warm and sunny. Vicki and the twins had taken the huge sail out to the lawn between the house and the canal. They had spread it out fully and were now walking slowly around it, examining it for the best spot to cut the sabot sail. Vicki had Bob's old sail in her arms.

The regatta was a week from tomorrow. It would be close, but if Tak helped her this weekend, she'd make it.

"Here's a good place!" said Misao standing at the foot of the big sail.

"How about over here?" countered Kimiko, not to be outdone by her sister.

Vicki surveyed the two places. Misao's was the best,

Vicki and the twins had taken the huge sail out to the lawn.

the fabric seemed less worn and it had a seam in just the right place.

Vicki continued around the sail until she stood beside Misao. Then she shook out the sail in her arms and laid it over the one on the ground. Carefully, she maneuvered it until she had it in the best possible location, making sure the lines were straight.

"That's it!" she said. "Go get the scissors."

Misao ran for the house.

It was going to be a long job. The sail had to be cut, seamed and edged. The batten pockets had to be sewn on separately, and there were a million other little details.

The door slammed, and she looked up expecting to see Misao and ready to tell her not to run with the scissors. Instead it was Tak.

"Hey!" he said coming toward her. "You got it! Will it work?"

She nodded. "Look . . . There's plenty of room."

"Great!" said Tak. "Now you'll make the race."

"Maybe," she said. "If you help this weekend . . ." She saw his face cloud and stopped midsentence.

"I can't. Mr. Burns wants me."

"But . . ."

"A four day cruise!" he said, excitement beginning in his face. "This time I'll be second mate!"

"Oh, Tak! That's wonderful!" she said, forgetting for a moment her own disappointment.

"I'm sorry," he said looking down at the whiteness spread before them. "If it were an ordinary weekend—but this . . ."

"It's okay," she said smiling. "I'll manage."

Misao came back with the scissors, and Vicki began to cut, hiding her disappointment by carefully avoiding looking at Tak. He hunched down beside her and steadied the fabric.

"They're going to pay me seventy-five dollars for the four days!" he said, "and I'll have a chance to learn to sail that big yacht."

"I'm glad for you," she said and her smile was genuine. "I understand, Tak. I really do."

"Thanks, lady," he said. "I hope so."

eleven

∾ That evening, Vicki sat at the desk at home trying to concentrate on her science report and nursing her disappointment over Tak's coming absence. It was a fine opportunity, one he shouldn't miss, but it was hard to take.

She was also pretending not to notice her mother stirring up a cake in the kitchen. Vicki's birthday was tomorrow. Sarah's spirits seemed unusually high. Vicki wondered if she'd gotten a raise or found a better job . . . or maybe she'd finally saved the money for the bus tickets to Arizona, but she was afraid to ask. If it was Arizona she didn't want to know.

There was a knock at the door. Mother and daughter looked at each other questioningly. Vicki shrugged and went to the door.

"Who is it?" she called. She heard familiar giggles on the other side, then a soft lilting voice.

"It's Mrs. Ito, Vicki."

Vicki's spirits soared and then sank in quick order as she opened the door. There they stood, arms full of packages. It was Mrs. Ito and the twins.

"Surprise!" cried the twins together.

"I hope we're not intruding," said Mrs. Ito. "The twins couldn't wait until tomorrow."

"Of course not!" Vicki managed, ushering them into the apartment. "Come and meet my mother."

Sarah dried her hands and came eagerly to greet them. Mrs. Ito handed her a bouquet of daisies.

"I'm so glad to meet you," she said. "I've wanted to come for a long time."

Sarah embraced her warmly. "I've wanted to meet you too. My daughter speaks so highly of you and your family . . . and these are lovely!" she said admiring the flowers.

"Vicki is a very fine girl," said Mrs. Ito. "She and her boat have made my children very happy."

"Boat?" Sarah's face turned a shade paler, and she looked questioningly at Vicki.

Before either of them could say anything more, Misao thrust a long slender package into Vicki's hands. It was wrapped in bright colored paper and tied with a ribbon. Its shape told what it was.

"Open it!" commanded Misao. "It's your birthday present."

Vicki managed a smile. "Why thank you, Misao, but tomorrow's . . ."

"Yes," said the excited child, "but open it now!"

Vicki sank into the sofa, the package in her lap.

"Won't you sit down?" said Sarah to Mrs. Ito. She indicated the only chair in the living room. The two women came over and sat, Sarah next to her daughter on the sofa.

"Here's another one!" said Kimiko thrusting a lighter rectangular package onto Vicki's lap.

"Open mine first," said Misao. "Open mine first!"

Vicki looked at the two excited children standing in front of her and tried to put aside her predicament. There was no use stalling. They weren't going to allow it, and it wouldn't help anyway. The truth was already out—part of it anyway.

"Let's see," said Vicki. She began to unwrap the long slender one. From the paper and ribbon emerged a brand new paddle, something she wanted very much and something she needed for the race.

"Oh, baby! It's beautiful!" she said, hugging the beaming Misao.

"Open mine!" shouted Kimiko dancing up and down in front of her.

With effort, Vicki avoided contact with her mother who sat beside her stiff and silent. Slowly, she began to take the paper off Kimiko's gift. Dark green canvas emerged at one end, and she tore the paper off the rest of the way.

"A life preserver cushion!" she exclaimed, hugging Kimiko and swallowing the sobs which threatened to expose her.

"Now you can race," said Kimiko. "Can we watch?"

"Of course," choked Vicki.

"This is very nice of you." Sarah's voice was strained.

Vicki looked at her now and saw all her fears realized and written in bold lines on her mother's face.

"We've been waiting until the boat was finished," said Mrs. Ito.

"I'd better put these in water," said Sarah as if suddenly aware of the bouquet in her hands. Vicki knew her reason for going to the kitchen was to get control.

"I hope we didn't bother you by coming," said Mrs. Ito.

"No," lied Vicki. "It's just that mother's not feeling well."

Sarah returned, a degree of calm on her face.

"Mrs. Banyon," said Mrs. Ito. "You really should come to my house and see the boat. When it first came, I did not think it could be repaired. But now it is beautiful!"

"That's nice," said Sarah.

"It was so good of Mr. Schaffer to let Vicki fix it. . . ."

"And we helped," piped Misao. "Didn't we, Vicki?"

"You did," said Vicki hoping her mother would hold back the storm until the Itos were gone. "I couldn't have done it without you."

"I got to paint most of the bottom," said Misao proudly.

"And I sanded the rudder all by myself!" said Kimiko.

"We have seen this boat come back to life," said Mrs. Ito. "I am so glad we . . ."

Sarah stood up and went to the closet for her coat.

Vicki was surprised. It was only seven-thirty. Her mother didn't leave for work until ten.

"I'm sorry," said Sarah. "I really have to go. I work nights, you know."

"Ah! I'm so sorry," said Mrs. Ito. "We must leave also." She stood up and started for the door. "Children?"

Vicki hugged each twin in turn and whispered a special thank you in each of their ears.

"Please. Come to my house and see the boat." Mrs. Ito was smiling cordially. "You and I will have tea."

"I will," said Sarah tightly. "I certainly will, and thank you for everything!" She stood, purse in hand in the middle of the room.

Vicki saw them to the door, said her good-byes, and closed it behind them. Then she turned to face her mother.

Sarah threw her purse on the sofa and tore off her coat.

"You sneak! You lying little sneak!"

"Mother . . . let me . . ."

"Explain? It's been explained!" Sarah's face was red and her temples were pulsing. "You deceived me from the beginning. Nursing! Hah!"

"But Mother, you don't understand. Give me a chance!"

"I understand. You lied to me. You never intended to give up sailing. *Never*!"

Vicki stared, dazed by the intensity of her mother's anger.

"Mother," she said, trying to make her voice calm. "How has my working on the boat hurt anything? My grades are up—almost all 'A's' now . . . even science, and you know how hard that . . ."

"Shut up, Vicki! Just shut up!" She rummaged in the desk drawer and came up with a plain white envelope. "See this? Today I made the last addition. We have the money to go to Joe's."

"Okay," said Vicki, "But first, tell me what I've hurt by the boat."

"Have you spent time on that boat?"

Vicki nodded. "Yes, but . . ."

"It was time better spent on something else. Have you spent money on it . . . or did you steal . . ."

"Yes . . . no . . . I mean I never stole. *I never stole!*" Vicki sobbed.

"Then you've used the money you earned." Sarah's voice was cool.

Vicki nodded.

"I thought you had most of it saved for our trip!"

"I've been paying the phone bill," said Vicki evenly.

"So what!" snapped Sarah. "That phone was your idea anyway. We didn't need it!"

Vicki's temper broke. "That's not fair, Mother!" she cried. "We did need it!"

"What do you know about fair!" said her mother.

"Well . . . if you weren't so pig headed, you'd be . . . you'd be . . ."

It was Sarah's turn to stare. "That does it!" she said

with forced calm. "I'm calling Joe." She began rummaging in the desk again looking for the number. "And my only concern about that job at the Ito's was Tak," she said into the drawer.

"Tak's my friend," Vicki said with dignity.

Sarah looked long and questioningly at her daughter, all sorts of ugly thoughts visible in her face. "How do I know that," she said. "You lied about the boat. How do I know you weren't . . ."

"I work for his mother," cut in Vicki. "I'm there every day. It's not like we go off . . ."

"You've spent your time working on that boat, I suppose!"

"Pretty much," she agreed, "and taking care of the kids. Bob Schaffer said if I had it ready for the first regatta, it would be mine! *Mine*! I could have had a boat of my own for . . . for almost nothing!"

"I see," said Sarah. "I see that your Mr. Schaffer is a fool."

Vicki stopped short. She never should have mentioned him.

Sarah continued. "He had no right to give you that boat or to promise you . . ."

"Leave him out of it!" sobbed Vicki.

"No! He's responsible. He'll hear from me . . . or from a lawyer!"

Vicki couldn't believe what she had heard. "You wouldn't!"

"I would!" said Sarah stonily, "and I will!"

"There it is!" said Sarah locating Joe's number and reaching for the phone.

Vicki turned her back and waited. She heard her mother dial, and then she heard the phone ringing in Arizona. All her worst fears were coming true. All the things she'd prayed wouldn't happen were happening.

Numbly, she heard her mother talking to Joe, making arrangements for the move. Arizona was no longer a nightmare. It was a dry, merciless, burning reality, and she was going there to live!

She'd be hundreds of miles from the twins, from Tak, and from the little boat so nearly finished now. Beyond that, she'd be hundreds of miles from the sea. She'd be landlocked!

Tears ran unchecked down her face. Her big dream hadn't been smashed as her mother had predicted. It had been torn away from her, senselessly, angrily.

She heard her mother talking to her.

". . . turn around and look at me!" Sarah's voice was cold.

She did, and Sarah continued. "It's settled. We're leaving a week from Monday."

Vicki's chin went up. "I won't go," she said flatly.

Her mother's eyes blazed, but her voice remained calm. "You don't have a choice."

"I'll run away. You can't force me . . ."

"What'll you do! Sleep on the beach?"

"Maybe. I'll find someplace. Don't worry."

"No. You won't. There are ways that I can prevent

it." Sarah paused. "But I won't have to. You'll go and you know it."

Sarah was right. When it came right down to it, Vicki didn't have a choice. She'd have to go. In desperation she grabbed her jacket from the back of the sofa and started for the door.

"Where do you think you're going!" said Sarah, a tinge of fear mixing with the anger in her voice.

"What do you care!" sobbed Vicki, defeated. "You know I'll be back!"

She yanked open the door and slammed it shut behind her. Then she ran—down the stairs, out of the apartment building, and down the dark street.

twelve

∾ Vicki stood in the Ito garage looking at the boat. No one in the house knew she was there. After she had left her apartment she had wandered for awhile, aware of nothing but her own thoughts. Then she had realized she was only a block away from the Ito's. She had come here to be alone and to try to come to terms with this thing that had happened tonight.

She was going to Arizona. Even if she finished the boat, even if it were legally hers, even if a miracle occurred and her mother agreed to let her keep it, she couldn't take it with her to Arizona. The boat belonged here with the sea, with Bob, or with some other young sailor.

She walked around the hull, running her hand along the polished teak. It was finished now except for the sail. She'd see that that was finished too. Now it was a matter of pride. She wanted to give it back to Bob complete, whole, restored.

And there was something else. He had said that when the sail was done, the boat would be hers. She wanted that too, if only long enough for her to paint on its stern the name that she'd been carrying in her mind ever since that first day on the *White Star*. When she stood at the bus depot in Phoenix, she wanted to know that the boat she had loved, that she had brought back to life, bore the name that she had given it. She deserved that much.

A degree of calm settled over her. She picked up the sail, sat down on the garage floor, and began to sew, making sure that the stitches were close and even.

She heard the garage door open and looked up to see Tak standing in the light of the doorway. He saw her tear-stained face and came to her quickly.

"What's wrong, lady?" he asked softly.

His gentle voice was more than she could bear, and the whole story came pouring out. He held her close as she talked, as if sheltering her against the cold and against the downward turns of fortune.

"Tak," she said at last, "I'm going to stay right here 'til it's done."

"You mean tonight. All night?" His face clouded.

"Yes, and tomorrow. However long it takes."

He shook his head sadly. "No," he said. "You can't."

"But . . . but why?"

Tak studied her face for a moment. "You just told me. Your mother's already threatened to sue Bob Schaffer."

She looked at him in disbelief. "Yes, but she wouldn't . . ."

"Wouldn't she? Think about how upset she is."

"But she doesn't even know I'm here. How can she be upset?"

"If you don't come home soon, where do you think she'll start looking?" he reasoned.

"She won't *start* looking," said Vicki defensively. "She has to go to work."

"But what if she doesn't go to work? What if she does come here?" he persisted. "Want to risk trouble for my mother, a lawsuit even?"

"That's ridiculous! She wouldn't . . . ."

"Vicki, be reasonable!" he cut in. "She would! She's scared. She's angry." He paused and looked steadily at her. "And there's another reason. If you stay here all night, she might. . . . Vicki you're a minor, you're not eighteen. She might even have some special charges for *me*!"

"Tak!" she cried in disbelief. "We haven't done anything wrong!"

"Want to try to prove that one?" he said quietly.

She looked at him in shock. How could he even suggest such a thing! In her anguish and confusion, the logic of his words escaped her. All she could think of was that he too had turned against her.

"All I want to do is finish this sail!" she sobbed. "What's so wrong about that?"

"Nothing," he said. "But you can't do it tonight."

"Then just leave me alone! Just go back in the house and pretend you never saw me!"

He stiffened and moved away. "I can't do that," he

said. "Even if your mother doesn't come, *I* know you're here, and *you* know it too."

The disappointment in his eyes over the intended lie made her flinch, but she continued, her anger mounting. "So!" she said. "You can't stay home from your precious cruise and help me, and you won't let me stay here and do it myself!"

"What's happened to you?" he asked, bewildered. "Suddenly you don't seem to care about anything but that boat!"

"And you don't care about me!" The words were out of her mouth before she could stop them.

"You don't mean that," he said, his face hardening.

"Yes I do! You know how much it means to me to finish that boat!"

"I'm finding out," he said bitterly. Then he turned, walked to the garage door, and stood there waiting for her to come.

"I think you'd better go now," he said finally.

"Okay," she said. "But tomorrow you'll be gone . . . sailing . . . and I'll be back."

He continued to stand quietly in the doorway, waiting.

"I'll go when I finish this seam," she said evenly. "Not before."

Tak nodded. "I'll be back in half an hour. Don't be here."

He turned away and disappeared into the darkness.

A cold wind came in from the door and bit through her jacket. She stared after him for a moment and then

*She stared after him for a moment
and then went back to the seam she was sewing.*

went back to the seam she was sewing. The fabric was tough. She tried several times to get the needle through, but her hands were trembling. Finally, she jabbed at it, and the needle went through the fabric and deep into her finger.

She pulled away and sucked on it furiously. Then she went back to the seam, but the finger bled, badly, all over the white sail. She tried to wipe it away, but it only smeared.

In desperation, she threw down the sail, snapped off the garage light and fled.

The alarm rang in the Banyon apartment at 6:00 A.M. Instantly, Vicki was awake and silencing its unnerving jangle. For once, she was grateful that her mother wasn't there. Last night, she had fallen into bed exhausted and slept. This morning her stiff and sluggish body rebelled against movement, but, as she dressed quickly in the near darkness, her mind was alert, her purpose clear. Step one: She would be gone before her mother came home.

Hurriedly, she let herself out of the apartment, locking the door behind her, and headed for the Ito garage. Since his cruise began at dawn, Tak would be gone. Today, no matter what, she would finish the sail.

All through the long Saturday, she worked. First the seams, then the mast sleeve, then the edgings. Detail after detail was checked off on her carefully made list. The twins came and went. Only once did she allow herself to stop—around one o'clock when Misao brought her a bowl of chowder. Only once did she allow herself to think about next Saturday, the day of the regatta, and what it meant.

Just as she finished mounting the wooden shoe at the top of the sail, Mrs. Ito drove into the carport. She got out of her car and waved.

"Ah. Vicki! It's done?"

Vicki nodded, and Mrs. Ito came over to inspect the sail.

"What a fine job!" she said. "You are a sailmaker too!"

"Do you think it'll hold?" Vicki was delighted at Mrs. Ito's praise.

"Yes. Of course it will. The stitches are fine and even." She paused. "It does need one thing—pressing. Bring it in." Without further ado, she started for the house.

Gratefully, Vicki followed with the sail in her arms.

Inside, they set up the board, and together they pressed the white dacron until the whole sail was smooth. Then they laid it out on the living room floor and folded it in the way Vicki had learned from Bob, so as to put as few creases in it as possible.

When they were done, Vicki turned to the small lady beside her. "Thank you," she said, her eyes saying more than her words. "You made all of it possible."

Gently, Mrs. Ito brushed a lock of blond hair from Vicki's face. "Don't think of it," she said. "You are almost like my own child . . . and now you are tired."

A warm glow crept over Vicki. No matter how long she lived, she would never forget this woman.

When Vicki took the sail out to the garage, it was almost dark. She put it carefully in the boat, and then she started for home.

That night, after her mother left for work, she sat at the table, her hands around a warm mug of coffee, studying the list her mother had left. Number one was "PACK" and scribbled next to it were the words "everything we don't need in the next week!"

Vicki stared around the room. Where to begin? The kitchen? As tired as she was, the kitchen seemed overwhelming. Her chest-of-drawers was handy. She wouldn't need all her clothes in the next week. She got up, dragged an empty box over to the dresser and in a matter of minutes had most of her things in the box.

What next? Her mother's clothes? No. Let her do that. But the bottom drawer of that chest was full of papers, documents. They wouldn't be needing those.

She got another box and opened the bottom drawer. On top were insurance policies, letters, her mother's marriage license . . . She read it. "Stephen Boyd Banyon," it said. It had been a long time since she had seen his name.

Under that was the picture of her father! All these years it had been right here in this drawer! She looked at it for a long time, memorizing the details of his face that the years had blurred and realizing that there were traces of that smile reflected in her own mirror. Then she placed it gently in the box and went on.

Next was her birth certificate, and then there was a document announcing final settlement of divorce between Sarah Virginia Banyon and Stephen Boyd . . . divorce? Vicki stopped short.

Her father was dead! She was sure of that. She even remembered the midnight call about an auto accident when she was very young and her mother's tears.

But here was proof that there had been a divorce. Her father had signed this paper in the same bold hand that he had used to sign the marriage license.

Then she read on. "Occupation: Merchant marine." The sea! Her mother's hatred of the sea!

Sunday was clear and crisp. Yesterday's wind had cleaned the air, and now the sky's reflection was almost turquoise in the canal. It was noon, and Vicki and the twins were in the garage admiring the boat.

"Let's see if it works!" said Vicki. Both twins nodded eager agreement.

Together, they rigged the boat. Vicki held the mast while the twins fitted the sail over it, and all three helped place it in the boat. Then they attached the sail to the boom and stood back.

In spite of her resolve, a lump rose in her throat. She forced it down. She watched the breeze ripple across the sail. The boom tossed gently back and forth. She closed her eyes and tried to imagine what it would look like in the water.

"We did it!" she said to the twins.

"It's done!" said Misao.

"Let's have a party," said Kimiko.

Vicki nodded. An event as monumental as this certainly called for one. "What shall we have?"

"I know," said Kimiko and disappeared toward the house.

"Why are you so sad, Vicki?" Misao had peeked behind her happy face.

"I'm not sad," Vicki lied. "The boat's done, for heaven sake! I couldn't be happier."

"Misao," yelled Kimiko from the porch. "Come help!"

Misao looked up.

"Go on. Help your sister make the party," said Vicki.

Suddenly she wanted to be alone with the boat. Even the company of the twins was too much.

She walked around the stern and drew up a stool. Then she took a piece of chalk and carefully wrote the name she'd been holding in her mind. She stood back and studied it a moment. Then she opened a can of black paint, stirred it, dipped the brush and carefully covered her chalk script with black paint.

The boat was finished. It was ready to sail. Tears brimmed until she couldn't see the lines she was tracing. She brushed them away and continued. The twins would be back soon. She wouldn't spoil it for them.

If only Tak hadn't turned against her, she could have borne it all—even losing the boat.

Misao appeared at the door carrying a heavy tray laden with three small cups and a large pot. Behind her

Kimiko carried a tray of rice cakes, small plates, and napkins.

"In a minute," called Vicki. "Don't come until I'm finished."

Carefully, she finished tracing the last three letters while the children spread the picnic on the grass just outside in the sunshine. She put the brush in the coffee can full of thinner and motioned for the twins to come.

Both children scrambled back to where Vicki was standing and looked at what she had been doing. The black letters stood out boldly against the teak. Vicki felt Misao's hand slip into hers and Kimiko's arm go around her waist.

Across the stern of the sabot were the words *The Passing Breeze*.

In her mind, she heard Bob's voice. "That's it, Vicki. Catch all the passing breeze!"

She had caught it, and now she must give it back.

She looked down, dry-eyed, at the twins. "Like it?" she said.

"It's great!" said Kimiko.

"It's perfect!" said Misao.

"Come on," said Vicki. "Let's have that party!"

They walked past the hull of the boat, out into the sunshine, and sat down on the blanket. Misao, anxious to play hostess, picked up the teapot and began to pour.

"When can we sail it?" asked Kimiko.

"Soon," said Vicki. "The regatta is this coming Saturday. After that . . . maybe Sunday . . . I'll take you out."

"How will we get it to the water?" asked Misao.

"Bob will come for it," said Vicki.

"Can we come too?" asked Kimiko.

"Certainly. We'll all go." Vicki was finding it hard to field the twins' questions. She would never sail this little boat. None of the things she was so glibly promising would ever come to be. She might not even see it in the water.

"I've got an idea," she said. "Bob says as soon as I get some racing experience he'll let me teach his junior class. You kids can join!"

"Can we race too?" asked Kimiko, the brave, the daring, the fearless.

"Of course," she said smiling, "but first you have to learn to handle the boat. There's a lot to keep in your head at one time."

"I don't want to race," said Misao. "I just want to ride."

"That's okay too," said Vicki. "Won't it be fun?"

Both children nodded.

Fairy tales, thought Vicki. I'm telling fairy tales. But she couldn't bring herself to shatter the moment with reality. Later this week, after the boat was gone, would be soon enough.

She sent the twins inside with the tea things and turned her attention to the boat, rigged and ready. She really should take down the sail, but she wanted to come back here tomorrow afternoon and see it just like this. She reached above her head and slowly pulled the garage door down. There. No wind would disturb it now.

She went into the house, said good-bye to the twins and Mrs. Ito and went home.

All day Monday, she thought about the boat and about Tak and about her mother. As soon as she got to the Ito house, she would call Bob and ask him to come for the boat. She hoped he would do it during the day. She didn't want to see it go.

As she came toward the Ito house, Misao and Kimiko came out to meet her on the road—both children near hysterics. The boat was gone!

thirteen

∾ Vicki had to see for herself. She ran to the garage door, threw it above her head, and stared into the empty space. Her mind blurred and she felt dizzy.

"It's stolen!" cried Misao voicing Vicki's fear.

"Did you call Mr. Schaffer?" asked Kimiko.

Without answering, Vicki ran for the house and the phone, the twins on her heels. She dialed the Schaffer home. No one answered. She dialed again. Still no answer.

Please, let Bob have it, she prayed.

She looked at the faces of the twins. They were wide-eyed with fear.

"Was the garage door open when you came home?" she asked.

Both little girls shook their heads.

"Is anything else missing?"

Misao shrugged.

"Maybe Mr. Schaffer put it in the water?" said Kimiko.

"Let's go see," said Misao anxiously.

Hastily, Vicki scribbled a note to Mrs. Ito telling what

had happened. Then they locked the door of the house and hurried toward the marina.

Vicki's eyes were scanning the row of boats even before they reached the dock. No wooden hull was among them. The boathouse was locked, but they peered in the windows. The sabot wasn't there either. Bob must not have picked it up. Wouldn't it be here if he had?

They started back toward home more slowly now. The twins were quiet, one on each side of Vicki and each one holding her hand. They never held her hand. At seven they were too big. Now it was a gesture of comfort for Vicki. They walked on in the late afternoon sunlight.

At the entrance to the fishing pier, they met Zeek who was just coming back from the coffee shop carrying a steaming white styrofoam cup.

"Hi, kid," he said. "Haven't seen you in ages."

Vicki managed a smile and introduced the twins.

Zeek nodded. "Tak's sisters, huh. I heard you were looking after them."

"Zeek," said Vicki tentatively, "you know about the boat . . . Bob's sabot?"

Zeek nodded.

"You haven't . . . you haven't seen it today, have you?"

Zeek looked at her intently. "Why, no! I . . ."

"It's stolen!" piped Misao. "Somebody took it out of our garage."

"Sh!" said Kimiko.

Zeek shook his head. "I'll keep a look out," he said. "I did see Tak though early Saturday morning. He seemed upset. You kids have a spat?"

Vicki reddened.

"Fine boy, that Tak," said Zeek.

They said good-bye, and he headed on out toward the end of the pier. Vicki and the twins continued on toward home.

Fog was setting in when they arrived at the Ito house. It was good to be in out of the chill air, to smell the familiar ginger and feel the warmth of the friendly room.

Mrs. Ito heard them at the door and came in from the kitchen, her face lined with worry. "Did you find it?" she asked.

Vicki shook her head, and the twins burst into tears.

Vicki knelt and hugged them close. "Don't worry," she said firmly. Then to Mrs. Ito, "I'm going home now. If you hear anything, will you call me?"

"I will. I'm so sorry!" she said. "I wish we had put locks on the garage doors."

Misao had an idea. "Maybe that guy next door took it. He was here again the other day."

Vicki remembered the strange man who had visited them.

"Maybe," said Vicki. "First though, we'll talk to Bob."

Sarah was asleep on the sofa when Vicki came into the apartment. She roused at the sound of the door closing and brushed a lock of hair out of her eyes.

Vicki stood at the door, her hand behind her still on the knob and stared at her mother. Sarah sat up, wrapping the cover around her as she did, and stared back.

"Mother," said Vicki firmly, "did you call Bob Schaffer?"

The smile which touched her mother's lips had a smugness about it that caused the hair on the back of Vicki's neck to rise.

"Yes," she said. "I called your Mr. Schaffer."

A wave of relief swept over Vicki. "Did you . . . did he . . ."

"He said he didn't realize that you'd do anything as stupid as to take that boat behind my back." Sarah's voice rang.

Vicki knew Bob wouldn't talk like that, but she cringed anyway.

"Mother, I have to know what happened. The boat is gone!"

"It better be. I told him if it weren't gone by the time you got there this afternoon, I'd take a crowbar to it."

Vicki stared at her mother in disbelief. "Where is it then?"

"At his house. He called me after he picked it up just to make sure I knew." Sarah paused, then continued. "Put it out of your mind. Mr. Schaffer has his boat back, and we're leaving for Arizona."

Vicki came and stood beside her mother, a strange calm settling over her. "The boat was finished," she said. "It was *mine!*"

"So he told me, but how would you support it? It costs money to own a boat—lots of money." Sarah was defensive.

"That was worked out too. Bob was going to give me a job teaching his beginning class. It would have been enough. Sabots are small, Mother. They don't take up much room."

"I don't want to talk about it," said Sarah. "Go start dinner while I get dressed."

"But I do. I want to talk about it," said Vicki standing perfectly still over her mother. "You never even saw the boat. You never took the trouble to try to understand."

Sarah started to get up, but Vicki continued.

"Mother, people have to be free. *I* have to be free!"

"Yes," said Sarah tiredly. "Free to ruin their lives. Free to walk on other people. Free to desert the ones who love them."

Vicki looked intently at her mother's face. She really believed she was right. She really believed the boat was wrong for Vicki.

"You've won," said Vicki, "not because you're right, but because you're older."

For a moment she continued to stand looking at her mother. Then she turned on her heel and started for the door.

"Vicki!" There was real fear in Sarah's voice now, not anger. "Vicki, where are you going?"

"Out!" she said and slammed the door behind her.

She walked—past the rows of apartment houses, past the small shops on Washington Street, past the entrance to the pier. The lights on the pier were haloed by fog. She climbed the ramp and started toward the end of the pier.

A figure emerged from the fog just ahead. Vicki felt a twinge of fear. She had been cautioned a thousand times about coming here at night by Zeek, by her mother, everyone. But it was a couple seeking private time wrapped in each others arms and looking, in the mist, like one. She thought of Tak. How good it would be now to have him here beside her. She felt a stab of pain.

But there were so many hurts tonight it was hard to separate them. She walked on down to the end of the pier and stood wrapped in the mist.

How long she stood like that she didn't know. There were no answers to the questions in her mind, no reassurances for the hurts. She did know that no matter how far her mother took her, she'd find a way to come back. Maybe by then all the people she knew would be gone, but there'd still be the sea.

A fog horn broke the stillness. Maybe Tak's yacht coming back to port? But no. He wouldn't be back 'til tomorrow. Maybe a tanker announcing to another tanker that he was near.

She leaned against the boat crane and stared into the mist. Then she looked down. She could barely make out the small fishing dock below.

Ahoy, girl in yellow.

Ahoy, *White Star*.

Catch it, Vicki. Catch the breeze.

Bob's voice was almost real. If only . . . if only . . . No! She must put that aside now.

She wished she could talk to Bob, but he probably didn't want to talk to her. Her mother had spoiled that too.

From now on, she must turn her thoughts away from sailboats and a gentle young man and even the sea. Tomorrow her life would be different. That much she knew.

fourteen

~ Vicki stood outside the Ito house on the narrow alleylike street. It had been a painful four days, and today had been the most painful of all. It was Friday, and she had just said good-bye to Mrs. Ito and the twins.

She had not seen Tak since that awful night in the garage. All week she had purposely left before he got home, but tonight she was waiting for him. She had to see him just once more. She couldn't leave on Monday without saying good-bye.

She saw his slender form emerging from the twilight, and she stood half frightened, half expectant, as he approached. He saw her and halted three houses away. Would he turn away? Would he refuse to meet her? She couldn't bear it if he did!

Without realizing what she was doing, she started toward him slowly, her arms extended. Then he was coming toward her, almost running. He dropped his books on the ground and took her hands. Neither of them spoke.

Then Vicki opened her mouth and struggled to say his name, but her throat refused to work. He drew her close and folded her in his arms. She tried again, but no sound escaped.

"I know," he said. "I know."

He held her gently and let her cry. All the anguish of the last week poured out.

Then they walked together into the Ito yard and sat down on the grass. It was cold and bleak, but she didn't notice. Tak tilted her chin upward, and she saw that his face was calm, almost smiling.

"We have two days left in the bank," he said. "How shall we spend tomorrow?"

"Together," she managed, her voice husky with tears.

"Sure," he said. "Let's see. We could go fishing. Want to go fishing?"

Vicki nodded. "Anything," she said.

"We could have a picnic," he continued. "Want to have a picnic on the beach?"

"Tak . . . I want to . . ." She hesitated. "The regatta. If the boat is there, I want to see it . . . in the water."

"You sure?"

Vicki nodded.

"Okay!" he said matter-of-factly. "That's settled." He rose and pulled her to her feet. "Come on. I'll walk you home."

By mutual agreement Tak left her at the apartment house steps. She climbed them slowly and opened the door.

The room was in semidarkness, and her mother was curled up in the corner of the sofa, a magazine in her lap. She was staring at a spot on the wall where a picture had been. She looked toward the door as Vicki came in.

Vicki snapped on a light, nodded curtly in her mother's direction, and started for the kitchen. The cupboards were empty now and standing open, salt and pepper shakers, plates, silver—the few last minute necessities—set out on the counter.

Feeling her mother's eyes following her, she picked up a cup and turned toward the stove. A pan of soup was warming on a burner next to the teakettle. She made a cup of instant coffee from the still hot kettle, squared her shoulders, and went back to the living room.

"Mother," she said, sitting down cross-legged on the floor opposite the sofa and looking directly at her for the first time. "Tak and I are going to the regatta tomorrow."

She held her mother's gaze steady with her own and waited. It had been a statement, not a question. Her resolve to go, to see the boat, was firm, but if there was to be trouble, she'd deal with it now. She'd had enough of secrets.

"I see," said Sarah finally, fingering a page of the magazine. "What time?"

"Ten-thirty." Vicki made a conscious effort to keep any trace of defiance out of her voice. She didn't want to fight anymore. Her head throbbed, and the muscles in her arms and legs ached from weariness.

Sarah nodded, laid the magazine on the sofa cushion next to her, and got up. "Hungry?" she asked.

Vicki shook her head.

Sarah went to the stove and began serving two bowls of soup. "Come on," she said and added, almost as an afterthought, "while it's hot."

Vicki got up slowly and came to the table, relieved at her mother's apparent calm. Neither of them spoke, however, and she welcomed the silence.

The first mouthful of the tomato broth awakened an appetite she had not known was there, and she ate, refilling her bowl when it was empty. She felt her mother's watchful attention but carefully avoided the eye contact that would have led to conversation.

A little after seven, Mrs. Banyon got up and put on her coat. "I'll call you from work," she said from the door. "Be sure to lock up."

"Okay," said Vicki mechanically.

After her mother had gone, she washed the few dishes and left them in the sink to drain. Then she wandered back toward the sofa. The apartment was bare now except for the boxes stacked on either side of the door.

Vaguely she was aware that her mother had left earlier than usual, but she didn't care. Decisions were made. Arrangements were complete. Arizona lay ahead, sun-baked and desolate.

She sank into the sofa and began to turn the pages of the magazine. Bronze beauties selling suntan oil grinned up at her from sun washed beaches. Well dressed women in spotless kitchens proclaimed the glories of a new improved floor wax. An article titled "New Careers for

Women" insisted that . . . that. . . . She slept.

Her mother's routine call at ten barely roused her. She pulled off her clothes and fell exhausted into bed.

When Tak and Vicki arrived at the dock, the sabots stood rigged and ready, their sails crackling in the fresh wind.

"What a day for the race!" he said, holding tightly to her hand.

But she hardly heard him speak. There were thirteen boats at the dock, and one of them was made of wood.

She ran, pulling him along to where the little boat was moored. It sat unrigged and rocking, six sabots on either side. She touched the bow gently, running her palm over the smooth and gleaming surface.

Than she heard Bob calling to the others from the end of the dock. She looked up to see him standing there as usual, clipboard in hand.

She looked at Tak, who was kneeling beside her. The question in her eyes was evident.

"Go ask!" he said. "What can it hurt!"

He was right. Maybe she'd earned just one sail in this boat. She got up and went to stand beside Bob on the dock.

"Hey, sailor!" he said as usual. "Where you been!"

"Bob . . . I just wondered if . . ."

"If what?" he said abruptly.

Three boys came up with questions and pulled his attention away. She waited, her body shaking, while he solved their problems and sent them away.

"Bob . . . just this once . . . could I sail the boat?"

"Why not? But get to it. White flag's going up."

She waved at Tak as she hurried toward the boat-house to get the sail and gear. He met her at the ramp and they ran the rest of the way together.

Back at the dock, they began to rig the little boat. Her hands trembled over the lines and fittings. She lectured herself. Forget it's only this once. Pretend it really is yours. Make it last . . . make it last . . . make it last!

She struggled with the cleat that held the mainsheet. Then Tak's steady hand took the line away and deftly fitted it into the cleat. She looked at him gratefully and began to fit the rudder onto the back of the boat. Tak was right. Today was today. She would hold it there.

fifteen

〜 Tak held the mast while Vicki pulled the sail sleeve over it. Then, together, they fitted the mast back into the boat. Vicki was just fastening the foot of the sail to the boom, when she heard Bob calling her on the bull horn—something about the entry form.

She stood up and looked at the boat, rigged and waiting. Then she ran to Bob, and together they began the form.

Skipper: Vicki Banyon.

Owner: Vicki Banyon

She stared at the paper. "But . . . but . . . it's not . . ."

Without a word, he pulled another sheet of paper from under the entry form, placed it under the clip and held it out for her to read. At the top of the paper in bold capital letters were the words "TRANSFER OF TITLE." Unbelievingly, she read on.

> This is to certify that I, Robert Joseph Schaffer, do transfer ownership of one wooden sabot known as *The Passing Breeze* to Victoria Anne Banyon for the sum of labor and parts to

restore it to its original sailing condition. I further state that I have inspected the boat in question and find it completely to my satisfaction. Therefore, I do hereby renounce all claim to it . . .

The lines all ran together. She looked up at Bob's face for a clue. Surely he knew. But there he stood, grinning at her, as if nothing in the whole world had happened, as if the earth really hadn't opened up and swallowed her.

"Bob," she said quietly. "I can't accept."

"I thought that was our deal!" he said gruffly.

"It was, but . . ."

"Look, kid. The boat's better now than it ever was. Look at it."

Vicki glanced at *The Passing Breeze* held now at the dock by Tak.

"It's a classic," said Bob. "Probably worth three times what a regular sabot is worth."

"Bob," she said firmly, "my mother won't . . ."

"Why don't you ask her," he said nodding toward a pale woman in sunglasses standing a few paces away.

When Vicki saw her, her first reaction was anger. Was she here to stop even this small triumph? But her mother was smiling.

"Go on," said Bob, "but hurry! Blue flag's going up in one minute."

Vicki went to her mother, and the two looked cautiously into one another's face. Then her mother spoke.

"Take me sailing tomorrow?"

Dazed, Vicki nodded. "Then . . . then you understand?"

"I'm trying," said Sarah. "Your father was a seaman. He loved the sea too."

Vicki nodded, realizing fully the courage those last two sentences had required.

Sarah continued. "I was young, not much older than you are now. He was gone so much—weeks and months at a time. I wanted him with me! I thought if I gave him a choice he'd stay." Her voice broke, and she paused, struggling for control.

"Mother, I understand," said Vicki. "You don't have to talk about it."

"Yes. I do," said Sarah, her voice steady again. "It's time you knew. I loved him so much. I never dreamed he'd choose the sea. Vicki, you have to believe I didn't even know you were on the way!" She paused, but when Vicki started to speak she rushed on. "And so there was a divorce. He had to be free too."

Vicki hesitated a moment then asked, "Did he ever know about me?"

"No," said Sarah. "I never told him. I couldn't use you to hold him."

"But you told me he was dead," Vicki said softly.

"He is. That part is true. The accident happened when you were four. Until then, I never gave up hope that he'd come back."

Sarah paused and looked over Vicki's shoulder at the water. "When you started talking about sailing, I just couldn't handle it."

"But what made you change your mind?"

"You did."

"But how . . . those things I said were . . ."

"Hurtful!" Sarah breathed. "But they needed saying, Vicki. And after that Mr. Schaffer called, asked me once again to see the boat."

"Did you?"

Sarah nodded. "Yesterday, while you were saying good-bye to everyone, he picked me up and brought me here. Honey, when I saw what you had done in spite of me . . ."

"Blue flag, Vicki!" called Bob.

"What . . . what about Arizona?"

Sarah shook her head. "Last night after I left for work, I stopped at a cafe and drank at least a gallon of coffee. Then I went to the bus depot and turned in our tickets."

"But that night job. What will . . ."

"It won't be forever. We'll manage." Sarah held out her arms, and Vicki went into them gladly.

"Now go!" Sarah commanded, releasing her from the embrace. "We'll talk later. Right now I want to see you sail."

Love and understanding filled Vicki's heart, and she touched her mother's cheek lightly with her fingertips. Then she turned toward the waiting boat.

Tak was still standing at the dock holding the bow line. When he saw her face, his own broke into a smile. As always, there was little need for words. He knew what had happened.

She ran to him. "About those days in the bank," she said.

"A deposit?"

She nodded.

The kiss that followed was sweet.

"Vicki!" yelled Bob. "Get yourself in that boat!"

Tak held the boat steady while Vicki scrambled in. Then he shoved her off.

"Go on, lady!" he shouted from the dock. "Show 'em how!"

Expertly, she maneuvered the sabot out of the slip and sheeted in the sail. She felt the boat move forward and looked up in time to see the sail with its red wooden shoe emblem fill for the first time.

The sea sparkled all around her. Ahead and to the right were the two markers which indicated the starting line. Twelve white sails were already moving back and forth in back of it.

She passed the line going downwind. Then she brought the boat up on the wind. It handled just as she had known it would. It responded to her every move. It seemed almost like an extension of her own body.

She headed for the starting line on a starboard tack, moving fast, hiking out. The gun went off, and the race was on.

Three other boats were ahead of her at the start, but no matter. The outcome of this race was unimportant. She had already won. The passing breeze was hers.

She felt the boat move forward
and looked up in time to see the sail
with its red wooden shoe emblem
fill for the first time.

15429

F
DEN
D392c

Dengler, Marianna

Catch the passing breeze